pins and needles

University of Massachusetts Press, Amherst

PINS & needles

stories

Karen Brown

This is a work of fiction, and any resemblance to persons living or dead is coincidental.

This book is the winner of the 2006 Grace Paley Prize for Short Fiction.
The Association of Writers & Writing Programs, which sponsors the award, is a national nonprofit organization dedicated to serving American letters, writers, and programs of writing. Its headquarters are at George Mason University, Fairfax, Virginia, and its website is www.awpwriter.org.

Printed in the United States of America

LC 2007020375
ISBN 978-1-55849-617-0

Designed by Kristina Kachele
Set in Adobe Garamond Pro with Sansa Soft and Oceanus display by dix!
Printed and bound by The Maple-Vail Book Manufacturing Group

Library of Congress Cataloging-in-Publication Data

Brown, Karen, 1960–
Pins and needles : stories / Karen Brown.
p. cm.
ISBN 978-1-55849-617-0 (alk. paper)
I. Title. PS3602.R7213P56 2007
813'.6—dc22

2007020375

British Library Cataloguing in Publication data are available.

For
Mary Lee Brown

Are those the faces of love, those pale irretrievables?
Is it for such I agitate my heart?
—SYLVIA PLATH, "Elm"

acknowledgments

"Unction," and "Destiny" originally appeared in *The Georgia Review,* "She Fell to Her Knees" in *The Tampa Review,* "Breach" and "Pins and Needles" in *EPOCH,* "The Ropewalk" in *StoryQuarterly,* "Apparitions" in *Ascent,* and "Dead Boyfriends" in *The Alaska Quarterly Review.* "Galatea," winner of the Crazyhorse Fiction Prize, will appear in *Crazyhorse,* no. 27 (2007).

I am grateful to the University of South Florida Creative Writing Program, my fellow writers and teachers, especially John Fleming and Rita Ciresi, as well as Tom Ross and Bob Pawlowski, who were there from the beginning. Many thanks to the editors who provided space for my work in their fine journals—Michael Koch, T. R. Hummer and Stephen Corey, M. M. M. Hayes, Ronald Spatz, W. Scott Olsen, Kathleen Ochshorn, and Lisa Birnbaum. Special thanks to the Association of Writers and Writing Programs, to *Sugarspoon,* for "Pins and Needles," and to my husband and family, for time.

contents

pins and needles

unction

They gathered each morning at seven o'clock in the bookbinding machine shop, in the back where the parts were stored in long, narrow, metal bins and stacked on metal shelving to the ceiling. Fans spun the dusty heat. They drank cups of dark coffee. They moved, their teenaged bodies dull and inarticulate, to the plywood counter where thick sheaves of computer printouts listed the parts they needed to count. It was a summer job, this inventory. Lily was pregnant, seventeen, and no one knew, not Orlando, the young draftsman, who taught her to drive his Renault, or Tish, the owner's niece, who brought in bags of the watermelon candy Lily secretly craved, not even Matthew, with his soft hair in his eyes, with his bashful glances that made her feel a part of herself had come undone, a blouse button, the clasp to her shorts, the silent, swift unraveling of her heart.

She could not tell you, now, who the father was. There had been a succession of boys at the time. She would leave her parents' house and walk the three blocks to the center of the small town, to the outdoor mall and its fountain, onto the town green's damp evening grass, and meet her friends, and wait for the boys. They would appear like gliding birds in their cars, paint jobs shining from a new waxing, the tires thick and ready to grab the parking lot's black asphalt. They stuck their heads out of car windows, their hair wet from the shower, from a quick swim in oval-shaped pools, from the lake in Suffield where some of them skied and a few would die in a boat accident the following summer. They lived without any fear of death. They grinned and promised a fearlessness that she desired more than the inexpert movements of their hands on her body, their mouths' wet urgency, their rising heat beneath her sliding palms.

They never forced themselves on her. She was practiced at how to make them want her. It became a simple game. Each boy was a new beginning. Each had an eventual parting, signaled by a new girl in the passenger seat of his car or a general disregard that she learned to intuit, never an angry rebuff, never with any malice, just a folding away of himself from her, a closing-off that made her sad at first. She would remember the smell of his upholstery, the salty taste of the skin on his throat, the way his mouth opened, or how he used his tongue. She would pine for the places they parked: the meadow beyond the reservoir, the smell of the grass dampened by rain. She would miss his groans, his efforts moving inside her, the way he fell panting afterward. She held all their faces the same in her hands. She gazed into their eyes. They all had a way of not looking back, of shielding themselves, as if from the force of her love.

The father of her child might have been any of them from that spring or early summer. She did not know for sure about herself until the end, in August, when the heat in the machine shop was the worst, and the black grit settled grimly on the handrails of the tall rolling ladders they moved up and down the aisles of shelving, seeking out the parts. Her breasts hurt. She drank her coffee in the morning and promptly threw it up. Only Matthew noticed, waiting outside the ladies' room for her, the worry in his eyes something they pretended wasn't there. He would brush her hair from her face. He would grin wildly to make her smile. In the afternoons he would sit on one of the high ladders and draw caricatures of all of them or the comic book superheroes he created. His body, large and ungainly, would curl in on itself, double over. His arm bent along the wide, white paper moved lithe and supple, like the appendage of someone else. He would present the drawings to her rolled up into long tubes, paper-clipped at the ends. She sensed her happiness was, to him, of the utmost importance.

There were six of them that summer, hired to work the seven-to-five o'clock inventory. At first she did not spend much time getting to know any of them. She took her list and went off into the aisles, working to decipher the language of screws and pins and bolts and clamps. She found time went faster this way. At lunch, she bought a sandwich from the truck that parked in the lot. The machine shop used to manufacture the bookbinding machine parts, but it had been closed for two years. Only a husband and wife ran the shipping department. There was Matthew, hired to build the wooden crates, operate the forklift, and pack things up to ship. A few machines remained operable. Two men ran those. Most parts were made in another of the owner's factories down by the Connecticut River—a bigger, more efficient place. The sense of the small bookbinding machine shop was of desolation and decline. Its dirt and grease, ground into the brick floor, were ancient, from another time. The sun lit the high row of narrow windows filmed by dust, turning them a pinkish orange. There was no other source of light beyond the hanging fluorescent lamps. Each morning Lily came into the heat of the shop and felt a new, raw wave of despair.

They worked without any supervision. After a week they grew bored. There was no one to please with their progress through the stacks of computer printouts. Lily knew that up in the front offices women in accounts receivable gossiped and split blueberry crumb cake, and purchasing agents lounged in each other's offices, sipping from cans of soft drinks, tipping cigarette ashes into cupped palms. The office manager carried on an affair with a file clerk, the blinds to his office drawn, and a receptionist sat at a switchboard by the American flag in its stand facing the double glass doors, waiting to greet the mailman. There were foreign engineers, three of them, spread out in cubicles, their suit jackets draped over the backs of their chairs, their drawings clipped to slanted tables, their ashtrays spilling over with the ends of hand-rolled cigarettes.

That summer, none of the office workers ever came to the back, except for Celie, one of the purchasing agents, who checked on things occasionally. She wore bright floral skirts and high heels and dangling earrings. She seemed uncomfortable in the dark shop, as if she might become soiled. She would stop in at shipping with her stack of paperwork, and then head to the other end of the shop, where the parts were kept, where by the second week the six of them sprawled on the metal steps of the rolling ladders, sat in folding chairs around the computer printouts, pretending to look busy. Orlando had the best performance. He would hold the printout like a book in his arms and thumb through it. He kept a pencil behind his ear and always seemed to appear from around a shelf at the appropriate moment to report in to her.

"We've got all the Rounder Backer parts accounted for," he'd say.

Celie would smile at him, making a special effort. Her earrings shook and made a sound like small bells. "Wow!" she'd say, shaking her head. "Good."

Orlando had applied as a draftsman just out of trade school. The summer inventory was the only job open, but they had emphasized there was potential to learn and the possibility of a later position. In the beginning, Orlando worked to entrench himself. He brought the engineers samples from his family's bakery. He made a round of the front offices daily, presenting himself as an affable employee. Lily begged driving lessons from him. She knew he would have to steal time from the company he was trying so desperately to join, that he did not want to do it. But she saw, too, that during that summer there was something about her that no one could refuse. After lunch, they drove in circles around the empty back lot where the machinists used to park. Orlando gripped the door handle when the car jerked and stalled. Sometimes he cried out in Portuguese and put his hand over his heart when her foot confused the clutch and the brake and she came too close to the shop's brick wall. Lily liked the smell of his car, the afternoon sun warming up a mixture of talcum powder and the baked crust of the bread he'd brought in that morning. She liked the way she could confuse him, how in the little car with her he stammered, no longer the expert.

During work hours Orlando was the only one who could describe the parts they sought, their size and shape, what to actually look for in the narrow bins. But by the third week of inventory they grew weary of consulting him, and they counted anything, their hands oily from the screws' threads, gray with dust from the castings piled up on the floor, their part numbers raised metal that no one, in the dim lighting, could truly read. If it looked like a lever arm, Jamie said, then it was the lever arm on the list.

Lily suspected that Jamie was working, like she was, as some form of penance. Lily had been hired in the shop's front office that winter. She got the job from her school disciplinary counselor, who met with her one afternoon after she had been discovered inebriated in French class. It had been French V, Advanced, and the other students, with their straight-A averages and bowl-shaped haircuts and polyester button-downs, had been shocked. Madame Dorn had led her by the hand out of the room. She had chastised her in French. "You disappoint me," she'd said. They stood in the beige brick hallway, on the pale and shining waxed floor tiles. Lily remembered the bright blue of her eye shadow, the way her small hands had clung to her wrists, the sound of the verb, *decevoir,* like an unending and upturned sadness. The disciplinary counselor was gruff and stocky with a broad face. He was missing half of one of his thumbs. He set up the interview with the bookbinding shop's office manager.

"You need this," he said. "Keep you out of trouble."

She worked every day after school making blueprints on the large machine. All the drawings of parts were stored flat in long, metal file drawers. She kept them in order, filed by their part numbers, some of them very old on tobacco-colored paper worn at the edges. She found that making the blueprints, the mindless feeding of drawings into the big machine, its heat and hum and ammonia smell, kept her content, and she was grateful, in a way, for the job. When they'd assigned her to the summer inventory, she found she'd become good at accepting whatever she was given.

Jamie had been hired under similar circumstances through a friend of his father's. A safe occupation for the summer. He wasn't resentful. With his checks, he claimed, he would put a down payment on the Trans-Am his father had already refused him. Jamie kept his blond hair cropped short. When he looked at Lily, his eyes lingered, needy and intent, on her face, her mouth, the slope of her shoulders down to her breasts. Tish came in each morning, primly, in a different colored sleeveless blouse, carrying her canvas tote bag. Her father wanted her to learn the value of hard work, she told them, crossing her brown eyes. She would leave each afternoon, her face shining, her blouse ringed with sweat under her arms. The other girl working with them, Geri, was tall and had a long, bushy mane of hair that she spent time twisting and piling and clipping back. She wore her boyfriend's UCONN T-shirts. Even these, Jamie announced, could not hide the bouncing effect of her large breasts. Geri was good-natured about Jamie's observations. She stuck her tongue out at him and disappeared down an aisle of shelving.

"Do you think she wants me to follow her?" he would ask Lily. "We could fuck in D row, under the Smyth sewer bolts." Lily and Jamie did the least amount of work. They sat at the plywood counter amidst the printouts, rifling through them, organizing them, pretending to mark things off. They separated the work into piles for everyone. Jamie smoked Camels, dropping his butts on the floor and grinding them with the toe of his boot. He looked over at her.

"This is unendurable," he said, his eyes fastening on her bare legs spread out under the counter. She looked back at him, and shook her head, refusing him, her body taken over by an inexpressible lethargy, an emptying of desire. She felt drawn into a current of deep and swirling water. No one seemed angry that she did less work. Matthew wheeled the big ladders around for her. Tish brought her the watermelon candy. Matthew and Orlando, finally, unbolted the green vinyl couch from the break room's linoleum floor. They carried it to the back wall of the shop, beneath the high row of windows, hidden away behind the last row of shelves. They said it was for everyone to take turns. Jamie offered to double up with Geri. But they relinquished it to Lily, who fell asleep every afternoon, her eyelids heavy, her limbs lifeless, her body drawn under invisible tidewater.

Once in a while, the Russian engineer would saunter through the shop. He would make a point of walking over, stopping, and asking for Lily. He needed a blueprint made. He couldn't find a drawing. He wore his dark suit pants and polished shoes. His shoe leather creaked, making his footfalls menacing. Matthew's face reddened when he saw him approaching. They made up excuses so Lily would not have to speak to him. That spring, the engineer had asked Lily to model, to pose wearing a nautical shirt and white shorts and a sailor's hat, with a bow thruster he had developed and patented for the owner as a side job. She had agreed, flattered at first. Celie in purchasing had done her makeup in the ladies' room. The engineer had taken the photos himself with a Nikon. He stood, stiff and unfriendly, issuing orders. He had her straddle the design, something that looked like a heavy, riveted pipe. Then she stood up beside it with one hand on her hip. Frustrated, he gripped the fleshy part of her arm above her elbow to position her, and his thumb and forefinger left a darkening print.

They took the photos in the machine shop. The late afternoon shone serene and unconcerned through the high row of windows, and the dust swirled about. She was not ready to reveal to the adult world her own knowledge of sex, and so she pretended she did not read anything in his eyes' movements over her body, his positioning of her, roughly, in poses of his liking. She could endure his gaze under this pretense, her hips and mouth prodded to assume falsely, awkwardly, the expression of seduction. Later, the engineer tried to persuade her to attend a trade show with them in Boston and hand out brochures, offering to pay for her hotel room and traveling expenses. But the office manager intervened, pointing out that she was a minor, and Celie had taken her aside. "Don't go," she'd said, grimacing. "I wouldn't if I were you," fully convinced of Lily's ignorance concerning the engineers in their suits, their thick waists and formality, their other uses for her they were not telling. The engineer improvised with a photo made into a life-sized cutout to stand alongside their display—Lily in her sailor's hat, a hand placed on her outthrust hip, her look conveying a disarming innocence.

Matthew had been in the shop during the shoot. They took the photos once everyone left for the day, and he stayed under the pretense of working late, suspicious of the engineer's intentions from the first. Later, he drew a scathing caricature of the Russian holding his camera, his oversized head stern, his one exposed eye, sly and lascivious. During the summer inventory, Matthew drew a whole series of characters. They were heroes from fantasy stories, men and women who had survived the last battle on earth and now fought latex-suited foes from space or mutant animals, lion-mouthed, vulture-winged, who inhabited earth's dark recesses. The human survivors wore only remnants of their old clothing. Their nearly naked bodies swirled in motion, spun on muscled calves, swung weapons that looked cumbersome and medieval. Their faces tightened in anger or horror or pain. Their eyes glared or softened or filled with tears. Matthew would bring the drawings to Lily, shyly, when the others weren't around. She had never seen anything so beautiful emerge from a pencil on paper before. She held the drawings and her hands shook. The characters looked back at her from the tumult of their movements, frozen in the midst of their unfolding stories.

She wouldn't say much. She would hand them back and look at him and smile, and she could see he knew what she felt, that she believed his ability was a gift, something that resided in some self other than the one maneuvering a forklift, stacking castings on wooden pallets, searching out 105 casing-in bolts. His caricatures of all of them brought out their beauty, the small defect in each of their personalities—Orlando's simpering and debonair nose; Tish's crossed eyes and self-deprecating smile; Geri's horsey face, its lack of imagination; Jamie's rakishness, a Camel hanging from his bottom lip. Of herself, Lily could only sense a kind of tragic weakness, her eyes too wide, too seemingly childlike, and she believed he had gotten her wrong. He would not draw any others of her, only real sketches he would not show her until later, near the end of the summer.

The notes came first. They were Lily's idea, grown out of the impossible state of her body, its languidness, its inconceivable separate heartbeat. It had been late afternoon. She had been asleep, and it had begun to rain. The rain on the shop roof was like something rising and building to a heightened pitch, the sound of it hollow and metallic. It woke her, and its thrumming made her lonely. She felt slighted by the condition of her body, as if it no longer had any other use than the one that now occupied it without her permission. She came around from the back of the rows of shelving and found Jamie with his cigarette at the counter. He gave her a look and then glanced over at Geri moping on one of the ladders, her fingers flaying her hair.

"I like that big head of hair," he said. "I want to put my hands in it."

Lily tore a piece of the computer printout. She wrote down his words with one of the pencils, in cursive script. "Put it in a bin on her list," she said.

"Add something else," he told her, grinning.

Lily wrote what she believed Jamie would want from Geri, what he wanted to do to her. *I can't keep this a secret,* she wrote. *I am overcome with lust.*

Jamie stubbed out his cigarette. He looked over Geri's abandoned list, and took off down the aisles. She didn't find the note at first. They watched her, waiting. They went off with their own lists, keeping an eye on her. Lily climbed to the top of a ladder and found the heat had collected there. She took the bin down to the floor and spent the afternoon counting and losing track and recounting 320 feeder nuts, finally placing them in piles of 25 on the brick floor. At the end of the day lining up to punch out, they noticed Geri's face, flushed, distracted. Tendrils of her hair stuck to her forehead. She said nothing about a note. But Lily saw her eyes take in the fine sheen on Orlando's dark skin, the way Matthew's pants had slid down on his hips. She saw them sweep across the broad space between Jamie's shoulder blades. Lily saw her wonder what his back looked like without his shirt. In her eyes was lit a kind of startled heat.

The notes, unsigned, unmentioned, would become the mystery that kept them searching in the bins of parts. Lily wrote confessions of desire and Jamie placed the notes in bins on everyone's list. *Yesterday, I couldn't breathe, watching you,* and, *I want, more than anything right now, to taste your mouth.* There was a certain stealth required, a cruel urge to unsettle and disconcert. Tish came to work in lip gloss, which she reapplied every hour or so, her thin lips glimmering and suddenly soft. Orlando grew a small, slim mustache and wore sleeveless tank tops. Geri arrived one morning in a halter, her breasts pressing the V of the front, spilling out over the edge of the fabric. Jamie leaned back in his chair, ecstatic. Lily ate the watermelon candies, placing them one after another into her mouth, letting them dissolve on her tongue, and wrote about what hands would feel like on someone's chest, sliding up a smooth stomach, riding down below the curve of a waist, the rise of hips, the warm, damp place between legs. She felt her body surge and slip into some region of wakefulness, a kind of knowing that mixed with the smell of the oiled parts, the paper and ink of the computer printouts, the artificial watermelon, the plywood counter where she piled the candy's cellophane wrappers.

Only Matthew seemed unchanged. He still gave her his quiet, thoughtful glances. He still waited for her in the mornings outside the ladies' room, his back pressing the brick wall, his arms folded patiently across his chest. He drew her when she least expected it. He would need only one or two quick looks, and those he would take while she was busy, unaware. Once in a while she would catch him and they would meet each other's expressions without knowing what their own reflected, hers sorrowful and lost, his fueled with love. Tish believed that Matthew had penned her notes. She came to Lily with them all smoothed out and pressed together, in a kind of order.

"Look at these," she said.

Lily looked. She already knew what messages they held. She had, she realized, intended for Tish to believe that Matthew had written them. She had mentioned his large Catholic family, the three sisters, the four brothers, the nieces and nephews, the value he placed on their closeness, the uncreased and simple sacrifice. Lily had thought they would make a nice couple. She had wanted Tish to pursue and capture him, to spare him from herself. In Matthew's notes she had written things she believed Tish might reveal. Her respect for her father's stringent rules, her mother's alcoholism, her loss, at fifteen, of a boyfriend to leukemia. Some of these were things Lily had learned. Others she had made up. She held the scraps of paper in her hands, and saw, through the disguised handwriting, the thoughtlessness with which she allowed the notes to lead lives of their own, assume their own history, their stories stretching out to contain moments that had not even happened yet.

"What should I do?" Tish asked. Her small lips trembled.

Lily shrugged, wordless with regret. Already, Jamie had tried to approach Geri and been rebuffed. Now, sitting at the top of her tall ladder, twirling her hair, Geri looked down at Orlando's head, bent counting over a bin, with a wistful longing. Orlando thought his notes came from Tish. He confided in Jamie, raised an eyebrow, and ran his tongue over his lips. "I can taste that gloss," he said.

Jamie became surly. "I'm done with this," he said. They stopped writing and hiding the notes. He sulked for three days, refusing to count anything, smoking his cigarettes and dropping his fist down on the countertop. The spell of the notes faded and was replaced with Jamie's irritableness. No one had the nerve to approach anyone else. No one knew how to feed all their wanting. Lily felt responsible, her own body, she believed, immune. But then she fell asleep late one afternoon on the green couch, and when she woke she could tell, from the slant of light, the way it colored the grimy brick, the gray metal shelves, that it was later than she'd ever slept. Matthew was there, near the top of one of the rolling ladders.

"I didn't want to wake you," he said. His voice floated from above her, resonant and strange. She knew the shop was empty, that everyone had gone.

"What time is it?" she asked. She imagined her mother waiting outside in the parking lot to pick her up, her exasperation, her refusal to go inside and inquire, the easy assumption that Lily had left with someone else. Now, she imagined her parents sat at the dining table, silent and still assuming that Lily was with a friend, or at the mall, or any number of places that Lily had invented in the past to appease them. Their cutlery clanked against the china. Her father glanced up occasionally as if to speak. In the flickering crystals of the chandelier, in the polished handles of the silver, the colors of the room bled, the magenta of her mother's blouse, her father's kelly-green golf shirt, the still brilliant but wilting centerpiece of flowers, all of it tinged with presentiment.

"I can give you a ride home," Matthew said. He descended the ladder. She slid over on the couch, and motioned for him to sit beside her. He hesitated, then dropped onto the vinyl cushion, casually, looking away. He let his hands rest on his thighs. She stared at the curve of his neck, his cheek. He would not turn to face her.

"Don't do that," he said, barely a whisper.

Lily could see the twilight slipping through the narrow windows, its sifted particles converging. She felt the air in the shop like a presence on her skin. She rose up onto her knees. She turned his face toward her with her hands. He was caught there, and resigned, he allowed her to look at him. His face stayed impassive. His eyes confounded her, like those of his characters. She slid her hands down his shoulders. She felt the tops of his arms, their hardened muscles. Her hands came to rest on his.

"Why didn't you write to me as you?" he asked.

She felt a conflagration of loss. She felt consumed.

He did not know, exactly, what to do with her. But he had a restless sense of what he needed, and how to get it. His mouth was soft and clumsy. His hands, large-knuckled, tentative, touched her face, her eyes and mouth, her nose and ears. They smelled of the oil from the bins. They settled on her body like a blessing. She felt the ache in her rise to the surface of his fingers. She had, she admitted, allowed herself to imagine this. She had even created the story of what might come after, his large family ready to take her in, to tend to her, to accept her body and its child as his. She saw bureau drawers layered with tiny, pastel-colored clothes, lamplight in an attic room, a window looking out into the ruffling dusk of waving leaves. She saw herself relent to this unfolding, her loneliness purged in soft breath and fine hair and the lulling scent of milk. But lying with him on the vinyl cushion, their hipbones pressed together, his need released, his love at her disposal, she felt only the betrayal, keen-edged, merciless, and knew nothing in her grasp would ever ward against loss.

She did not finish out the summer. He would never know how her body swelled, or didn't; how her breasts filled, or not. She kept only one of his drawings, that of herself just awakened on the couch. He drew it that day from above, on the ladder. In it, the twilight is a color on the brick. The vinyl couch casts its own darker shadow. Her legs are folded, one on top of the other. She looks up. In her eyes he has placed a perfect, earnest love. She leans on one arm and the other curves in a motion of possession over her abdomen. Everything, then, still part of the story.

she fell to her knees

Nell met him the first time she went to the house. He came across the backyard with his drink. His clothes were rumpled, as if he'd been lying down in them—a dress shirt, a pair of gray trousers. It was a weekday afternoon. They stood by the seawall and he asked her what she was doing there. The ice in his drink slid around. His eyebrows came together, laughing at her. He had sandy hair in need of a trim. He was the neighbor and had noticed her car. He could fill her in on a number of things about the house, he said. Take that tree, for instance. Nell noted the fine bones of his hand, gesturing, the way his sleeve slid up to reveal his slender wrist. He was younger than she, and in need of saving. He did not so much say this as attempt to hide it. She forgot his name as soon as he said it, and later, she had to ask.

Nell inherited the house from her mother's boyfriend, Vince Morrell. She had not seen or spoken to Vince since her mother's death when she was seven, and her initial desire was to decline the key. It was bronze with a cardboard tag and it dangled from the attorney's bright fingernails like something plain and easily resisted. Nell asked the woman to sell the house, but she talked Nell into visiting it first. "There may be something you want there," she said. "For your children." Nell's two children were grown now, and away at school, but the attorney made her feel she owed them something: a memento or a souvenir. Nell understood now how she submitted to the coercion—that the attorney's suit, its wool fabric fitted perfectly against her body, her pearls resting in the hollow of her throat, her scenario of a house holding a secret history that must be passed down, had all undermined Nell's wish to avoid the place and its contents.

She went to see the house on a Monday afternoon, driving thirty minutes on the interstate to get there. The neighborhood was announced by a wrought-iron sign—the name Sunset Park written out in ornate lettering. Nell had passed the sign on her visits as a child, every other weekend when her mother was alive. She did not have many memories of the house, and only a few of her mother, who had been denied full custody. In the 1950s, the twisted black iron curls established the neighborhood as lavish and upscale. Now the sign leaned, rusted and off-kilter, its tiered brick base sunk into layers of limestone and sand.

The house had not been difficult to locate. It was one of those long, rambling ranches, built of hollow block with bricks inlaid on either side of each window in the semblance of shutters. There were wrought-iron supports on the front porch, and a screen door with the outline of a flamingo. The roof was white barrel-tiled, slick with moss, blackened by mold. Azaleas occupied the front beds, rangy and almost leafless with a few early pink blooms. Grapefruit ripened on the tree in the side yard, the branches weighted to the ground with the neglected fruit, and through the carport Nell watched the open bay tremble under pale winter sun. The rest of the neighborhood was composed of new homes interspersed with bare lots of dirt, etched with tractor's tires, where other ranch houses had been razed. The new houses were large with Mediterranean influences—iron balconies, terracotta tile roofs, stucco exteriors painted yellow and pink and a color like beach sand. Built high off the ground to meet flood codes, they towered over the few remaining ranches in a way that made Nell feel uncomfortably part of the space of years that separated the aged doctors and lawyers from their younger counterparts.

Nell's mother's affair and the ensuing divorce had been scandalous for its time. As an adult, Nell admired her mother's audacity, but as a child, she had resented it. Nell stood outside the front door and found that her hand shook as it fit the key in the lock. She stood on the threshold and remembered how it had felt to believe that she had been overlooked; that in the larger picture of her mother's life she was inconsequential.. Once inside she felt the urge to leave the door open, to keep the outdoors and its humidity accessible, and prevent the smell of the house—dust and mold, the scent of burned linoleum, of charred plaster and ceiling rafters and plastic coated electrical wires—from invading her clothes. She went through the main rooms and opened all the windows, just glancing at the furnishings—the sofas and their sagging cushions, the tall, glass-beaded lamps, the wallpaper, damp and peeling from the walls, the horrible blackened hole in the kitchen ceiling. All of it made her apprehensive. She walked out through the den's sliding glass doors, down a small cement path through a stand of tall juniper to the seawall.

That afternoon, standing there, she met the neighbor. He told her Vince Morrell had set fire to the kitchen. Vince was old and incompetent, and finally a year ago was removed to a nursing home to die.

"That's too bad," she said, absently. The bay water hit the seawall with a languid slosh. Nell tried not to imagine big Vince Morrell, his darkly curling head of hair turned gray and patchy, his thick appendages whittled down to a helpless thinness. She had disliked him as a child because she believed he had taken her mother from her, and she felt sorry for this now. There was a slight breeze off the bay, warm and heavy. It was rancid, like the runoff silt filling up the canals. Nell could not admit a relationship to Vince or the house, so she lied to the neighbor and told him she had purchased it. He gave her an admiring look, as if she impressed him with her business sense, and then the look went on, Nell noticed, intending something else.

"I would invite you to sit down, but I don't know about the chairs," she said. The brick patio was grown through with tall weeds, and four lawn chairs were grouped in its center, their plastic seat slats dangling, their metal frames corroded with rust. The neighbor looked over at the chairs and smiled.

"Vince and I might have managed those a year ago," he said.

Nell did not want to talk about Vince. Behind her, through the open sliding glass doors, the smell of the house came out into the backyard.

"He was an interesting old guy," the neighbor said. "God, that was awful, watching them take him off. You know, all that struggling, having to be subdued. You don't want to watch that happen to anyone."

Nell stared at him. He looked a little afraid. "I imagine," she said.

He squinted and sipped his drink to the melted ice, and then he glanced down into his glass. "I like your eyes," he said. "They don't give much away."

Nell found she could not respond. She felt her heart quicken. The neighbor took a sip of his drink. He smiled at her with his wet lips. His own eyes were sad and greenish, like the bay.

"I don't suppose you have any gin," he said. He looked behind her, toward the house.

"We could see," she suggested.

He waited out by the juniper, and Nell went back into the darkened interior. She saw, in her search, a game of backgammon abandoned on a table, the Chinese screen she used to play behind, the chandelier dangling glass beads like her mother's earrings. Everything was covered with dust and cobwebs, acquired in the year since Vince had been removed, or probably before that, when he was too old to dust and clean. She crossed the slate floor in the family room to find the round cabinet filled with dusty bottles. She did not want to emerge too soon with the bottle, to seem that she had any previous knowledge of the place. But she wanted to return to the neighbor, to his empty glass and his rattling ice. She liked the idea of him waiting for her with his barely concealed need. It gave her a kind of power she had not felt since Sweeney, the man with whom she'd had an affair years ago, when her children were young. From outside the open windows came the smell of the bay and the grapefruit that had fallen to rot in the winter grass. When she went out with the bottle, the neighbor was gone.

———

His name was Teddy. He had lost his job, and was supposed to be searching for another. His wife, a pediatrician, crossed the driveway with her hand extended one afternoon as Nell emerged from her car.

"Are you the new neighbor?" she asked. She had a practiced composure. Her hair flowed thick and blond from its roots, down past her shoulders. Nell clasped her small hand. They told each other their names. Nell felt the wife's eyes take her in—her blouse, its small tear by a buttonhole, her faded jeans, her hair worn twisted back, her face without makeup, exposed and assailable. Nell saw her eyes feign interest for the minutes they conversed. Then they parted. Teddy's wife's heels clipped along the paved driveway, up the long set of stairs. Nell watched her disappear into the house. Later that day, Teddy stood outside the sliding glass doors and the breeze off the bay caught his collar.

"So, what did you make of her?" he asked.

"I'm not sure," Nell said. "What did she make of me?"

Teddy laughed. He shook his head at her, slowly, and would not answer. He shook the ice in his glass.

"I think she misjudged me," Nell said.

She slid the door partially open and stood in the gap. The smell of the house came out from behind her. It passed through her clothing like a specter.

Vince Morrell's roses still climbed the trellis along the side of the house; the lawn had become crabgrass and horse nettle with patches of dirt. The house had always seemed huge, and maze-like, its box hedges neatly trimmed, hiding the Easter eggs she and her mother spun around in coffee cups filled with vinegary dye. The azaleas bloomed pink and gaudy. There were parties by the bay on a brick patio, her mother in a long green dress and rhinestone sandals, smiling, showing all her teeth, her hair long and dark and held back with a barrette. Nell remembered the smell of Vince's Vantage cigarettes left burning in all the ashtrays, the crumpled packs wedged between couch cushions. She would go around and put the cigarettes out, the filters dented by the grip of his thumb and index finger.

Vince Morrell loved the Sunset Park house, and once, to hurt him,

Nell's mother called a Realtor and signs appeared, one in front facing the street, another in the back for boaters on the bay. The maid, Aurora, told her that the house's sale would be ensured if she buried a statue of St. Joseph, and so her mother told Aurora to just go ahead and bury one. Nell remembered Vince Morrell on the lawn one night, digging holes with a trowel, trying to uncover it. There had been drinks and arguing. Vince's glass sat on the walkway while he dug, the amber liquid shimmering in the lamppost light. Her mother had stood in the doorway, goading, calling out to him every so often to see if he had found it. Nell watched from her bedroom window. She smelled the metal of the window screen, the leaves of the azalea plants. It was Christmas then, too, the house trimmed with a row of lights that cast color onto the hedges. Her mother's and Vince's voices reverberated against the balmy silence of the neighborhood at two a.m. There had been other fights, suitcases thrown out onto the lawn, her mother in her robe wandering off, and then found, her robe translucent in the car's headlights. Nell never mentioned the turmoil of her weekends with her mother to anyone. Even as a child she knew to assume, as they did, the guise of normalcy.

The first time Teddy had come into the house he whistled through his teeth. He stepped carefully, his arms out a bit from his sides, as if he thought something would topple over and break in his wake.

"This is like entering a time warp," he said.

The house retained its original 1960s furnishings. Fabric had begun to give way—throw pillows, sofa cushions, lampshades, all worn or ripped or yellowed. The tables were spare shapes, their tops marked by the rings of Vince Morrell's drinks. The floors were oak parquet, warped in spots. The house's structural weakening showed in long cracks in the plaster ceilings and walls, in water damage that left wallpaper stained a color like dried blood. The kitchen, galley-style, had pine cabinets, worn down around the handles by years of Vince Morrell's grasping fingers. The roof's beams were exposed here, along with dangling wires and the air conditioning's metal ducts. Nell did not go into the kitchen with its injured ceiling. There were shelves in the living room filled with book-of-the-month club selections of the 1940s and '50s—Cozzens's *By Love Possessed, The Bedside Book of*

Famous British Stories, The American Character, Lin Yutang's *The Importance of Living,* and the *Fireside Treasuries* of short stories and humor and essays. Nell and Teddy looked through the books one whole afternoon. They sat on the parquet floor. They had one of the bottles from the liquor cabinet nearby and they filled glasses Teddy found in the kitchen cabinet and rinsed out in the sink.

"I hate warm gin," Nell said. She took a sip.

Teddy grinned at her over the rim of his glass. "Don't drink it then," he said.

Nell did not know if she liked him very much. The books were from before both of their times. They felt damp in her hands, the pages mottled and tinged brown at the edges. Nell would have liked to tell him how she once sat on the couch in this very room and tried to read them as a child, but she could not. Her deception made her quiet and hesitant. Next door, they heard a truck with a trailer pull up and a landscaper's crew run its mowers across Teddy's lawn. The smell of the books mixed with the scent of oil and cut grass. That day, the wind took the smell of the bay somewhere else.

Nell watched Teddy. He opened the books in his lap, carefully, flipping through the pages, looking up at her and shaking his head. He talked to her about each one, assessing it, giving his opinion. Nell felt his talking like a kind of mask over what they wanted from each other. After, she did not remember a word they exchanged. She had wanted to lean over the stack of books and place her mouth on his, and then she had done it, interrupting him mid-sentence. She felt his mouth, still shaped around the word he'd spoken. It tensed with surprise, and then softened. His free hand slid up along her face. The lawn crew cut its swath, the noisy mowers drowning out the sound of their sighing. The number of ways to kiss him unfolded. They stretched out on the parquet. He asked her, implored her, to remove her clothing.

"Just this," he said, undoing buttons. She put her hand over his and he stopped and groaned. The light in the room dimmed until they could make out only the glow of their clothes, the revealed places of skin. Outside the windows the lamppost left a halo of light on the front lawn. Teddy rolled away from her and stood, slowly, brushing down his shirtfront. He fumbled with one of the lamps and it lit the room the yellowed fabric of the old shade.

"Do you have to go?" she asked him. Nell could see the whorls of dust under the skirt of the sofa. Teddy looked around the room, flushed and amused.

"Why don't we move to a couch?" he asked her. He reached for his empty glass and tipped it back.

Nell propped her head in her hands. She grimaced.

"How bad could it be?" he said, and he plopped down on one and bounced. Nell stayed where she was, and Teddy smirked. "I assume there are bedrooms."

Nell had not been down the long hallway to discover them.

"I assume," she said. She felt the air from the open window. She felt her body on the parquet, a long seam of heat. The warmth rose out of her blouse. She thought he might want her to go to him on the couch, but she did not. She put her head back on the floor. She closed her eyes and heard the rush of air accompanying a car passing, a child's call from inside one of the houses, squirrels scrambling in the trees. She heard a grapefruit hit the ground, heavy and ripe. When she opened her eyes she was alone, resentful of his leaving her.

Nell had been coming to the house for over a month, but not every day. She kept her purpose for going there vague when she spoke to her husband, who had wanted to send a truck to cart off the contents, and who she only temporarily held at bay. Sometimes she brought boxes to fortify the pretense of packing things up or clearing them out. She was not sure yet, why she went. She liked the way Teddy wanted her, forcefully, without much talking. She craved his limey-tasting mouth. She thought she could make him want her enough to lure him away from his other life, to secure an admission of love. But then yesterday she saw two children playing in his driveway. One pushed a yellow metal truck, his bottom round in diapers. The other, a girl, and older, had a doll in a stroller. Both were fair-haired and dressed in bright, clean clothing. Nell watched them play from the confines of her car. The nanny, an older Latino woman, sat in a folding chair in the garage. She held a magazine in her lap and looked up from it occasionally to call out to them. "No, no," she said, and then some words in Spanish. The children understood the warning that came each time they approached the end of the driveway.

Nell remembered when her own two children were little, though she could not separate the memory from Sweeney. The long days of preparing meals, cleaning up spilled juice and crumbs, sorting pieces of puzzles and toys into their respective bins, changing clothing and diapers, the tediousness of her life, was charged, suddenly, with the memory of his mouth, her body sore with wanting him. He had been a swim instructor at the country club. For the time they were together Nell was troubled by desire. She would notice things like the striated colors in the sky, birds in formation shifting and wheeling, leaves blown across her windshield while she was driving, and feel them all like a violent longing. His body smelled of the heavily chlorinated country club pool. He lived in a small, shoddy apartment accessed by a wooden outdoor stairway. He left his towels on his bathroom floor to stiffen with mildew. When she left at dusk he would turn on the lamp by the bed and she would see him, the expanse of his bare chest, the taut skin that joined his hipbones, illuminated through the uncurtained window glass.

It hadn't lasted. He quit the club and she stopped hearing from him. She assumed, finally, that he had grown tired of her leaving him and found someone else. The summer of the abandonment, Nell went to the beach with her children to get away. She had not wanted to see her husband's happy, steady face, pouring his morning juice, humming to himself. She'd used her father's beach house on Anna Maria Island. All day the children had busied themselves in the warm sand. Nell remembered her despair now, how much it had bothered her to be forgotten. She would give the children their baths and put them in bed. Then, sitting by the water, she drank. The little waves came in. The coquinas dug themselves back under the sand. She awoke each morning with a headache, morose and silent. She could not understand it. Her life with her husband and children was a course of events already set in motion, impossible to breach. She would not, like her mother, abandon one life for another. Surely, it had been only the sex she wanted. There wasn't any absence of love, just his body missing from her life—his adoring mouth and hands, the light pressure of his hips, the simple way their bodies fit.

"I want him one more time," she'd whisper, an addict.

This time there were no children to occupy her, their little bodies under her hands, expectant and greedy for her ministrations. Now, there was only Teddy, his mouth wet with gin and lime and ice, his forehead scarred from the skate blade of a childhood hockey game, the mole on the inside of his arm, the sheen of sweat on his chest, the soft timbre of his pleading she could not refuse. She had begun to imagine them together other places, in restaurants she liked, at the beach house, on trips that she could easily pay for. But in the house she knew it was just their bodies and what their bodies did, and there would never be anything more than that.

Nell breathed the house's stale air. Its heaviness dulled her movements. Inside the front door was a plate of switches and she hit them all, flipping on a foyer light and the porch light and the lamppost on the yellowed front lawn, an ornate piece of wrought iron with three glass shaded bulbs. She went through all the rooms, opening up the windows, and then out the sliding doors where she saw Teddy was already waiting for her. Some days he did not come, and she would sit in the house on the old couch cushions, and remember the way she had, as a child, waited for her mother and Vince to return on the nights they went out. Out by the seawall, Teddy wore a white T-shirt with his trousers and his feet were bare, as if he'd partly undressed or made some kind of quick escape. He carried a bag of ice and his glass. He looked a little wrung out and sheepish.

"I forgot my shoes," he said. He wiggled his toes. They were white and chilled in the dead grass.

"Do you really need them?" she asked.

He shrugged. Nell had come later because, she told him, she wanted to see the sunset on the bay. He had mentioned it before, and she wanted to see for herself. She did not want to tell him the truth, that she had finally agreed to let her husband send the truck in the morning.

"I almost missed you," Teddy said.

They stood by the seawall, looking at each other.

"Did you think I wouldn't come back?" Nell asked.

Teddy stared for a long time at the base of her throat, then turned and glanced at the choppy bay, hiding his expression. Nell wore a sweater. She supposed he was cold, the way the wind came off the water, and blew his hair over his eyes. The bag of ice dripped into the dirt of the yard. Around them the wind bent the tall juniper so that it appeared to bow in reverence.

"Do you want to go inside?" she asked, though she did not know why. A formality, the way she would ask her husband if he wanted the newspaper when he came downstairs in the morning.

Soon after their first afternoon together, she and Teddy had gone down the dark hallway to the bedrooms. He had opened each door, and they had glanced inside.

"This must be little Jimmy's room," he said. He leaned in the doorframe. She stood behind him and wrapped her arms around his waist, slid her hand below the clasp of his pants. Over his shoulder she saw a twin bed with a chenille bedspread, and a pine chest of drawers. On wooden shelves stood trophies and models of army airplanes. This room belonged to Vince Morrell's son, Vince Jr. Nell remembered the smell of model glue coming out from under the door, how she would knock and ask to be let in, and he would refuse. He died in his twenties in a car accident on the causeway. She knew the room across the hall would be the one she stayed in, that it, too, would be the same—white French provincial furniture, a bed with a canopy like one she had pointed to in a Sears catalog, and her mother had sent Vince out to purchase for her.

"Little Sally's," Teddy said. He had flipped on the lights. The canopy fabric hung in tatters. Nell could still make out the pattern, purple stripes, like ribbon, and pink roses. The blinds on the windows that looked out to the road were bent. There was a large patch of spreading dampness on the wall underneath them, as if they'd been left open during a storm, and the rain had filled the sills and spilled over. Nell's mother's collection of horses still stood on the desk shelf. Nell had never liked them, their fiery faces, their heads rearing back to show dilated nostrils. She had thought the manes, soft real hair, were the only redeeming thing about them, but she had taken them from their boxes and set them all out on the shelf in a false show of devotion when her mother asked, with her sorrowful eyes, why she never played with them.

The room beside it was the master bedroom, darkened with drawn shades. The carpet was faded and stained. The bedcovers were kicked down, as if someone had just gotten up—a turquoise blanket and yellowed sheets. Nell had pulled Teddy back into the hallway, her mouth on his neck, her fingers undoing the buttons of his shirt. She had learned as a child, through overheard adult conversation, that this was where Vince had found her mother, overdosed on Seconal. She had imagined for herself what the adults would not say, that her body had been sprawled across the sheets, that there had been no pulse and nothing for the paramedics to attempt to save. Nell knew which robe her mother wore, the silver velour, slit up the front to reveal her long white legs. She saw her eyes, open and glassy, with their same questioning. *What?* she would ask, when she caught Nell looking. She would be on her way out to the patio with a drink, or dressed for dinner, her earrings caught in her hair. Nell would look away and say nothing. Not, *you are beautiful.* Not, *I love you.*

The last bedroom had been Aurora's. It held a twin bed with a bare mattress. The curtains were sheers, pulled back, and the light came in from the bay and wavered on the bare parquet. There was no other furniture in the room. Teddy lay down on the bed and folded his hands on his chest. He looked up at the ceiling, like a patient.

"Do something with me," he whispered.

She climbed up and draped her body over his.

"Say what you want," she told him, pinning his arms back, willing to give him whatever he asked.

On the last evening, Teddy followed Nell into the house. She felt his eyes on her legs below her skirt. She went to the family room first, to take a bottle from the cabinet, but Teddy dropped the ice and the glass on a table and took hold of her around her waist. He buried his face in her hair and exhaled, a long sighing breath. Nell felt a surge of panic and desire she tried to hide.

"What?" she asked him, drawing back.

This angered him, her cold detachment. "Stop it," he said, as if he might cry, or strike her.

He did not want a drink. He wanted her in the back bedroom, spread on the bed without clothes. He took her by the hand down the long, dim hall. Nell remembered Aurora coming out of her room in the mornings—her face drawn and pale, her dark hair like a hood in the shadows, her scuffing slippers. Her eyes softened when they saw her. She and Nell had gone into the kitchen together and made hot chocolate, warming the milk in a pan. Aurora let Nell stir. She remembered the heat coming off the burner on her arm, the metal spoon heating up in her fingers. Outside the sliding glass doors the bay was alive, skittish, changing colors. Nell's mother had gotten up next in her long silk robe. She stood looking at the bay through the doors. Her perfume smell hid in the robe's depths. Her hands stayed deep in the pockets. They came out to light a cigarette, and they shook.

"Do you like it here, Nellie?" she asked. Her voice was tentative and unsure. Nell saw now that her mother's love had been withheld in fear, waiting for a sign. That it might have poured from her, a liquid warmth, but Nell with her silence fended it off. She let Teddy hold her down on the bed. She let him slide off her clothing and cover her with his mouth and hands, with his own shaking limbs. When he was finished he rolled aside and pulled her up against his thudding heart. Underneath her the mattress was wet and cold, with a dank odor. They listened to the bay slap the seawall. They heard the voices of his children playing in the next yard. In the houses around them small and mundane things continued, the food preparing, the laundry folding, the sex in bedrooms, the safety of rituals tiding everyone over. Nell thought of her husband waiting at home for her, wondering about her absences, his plate of food on the table, his years of investment in her presence, and now, an empty house, her unsorted mail piled up on the counter. In the room with Teddy the sunset tinged the walls the color inside a conch.

"You will always have to go," she said. She looked down at his face, his eyes and their sad cast, his mouth saying her name. If all those years ago Sweeney had asked her to leave her life she saw now she might have done it. If her mother had once held out her arms to her, Nell would have gone there, too. She still did not know if she was spared or robbed. She looked down at Teddy's face and he watched her, wondering. She saw they would have love and terror, or they would have nothing. Nell felt her love for him, dire and urgent, like a hand over her mouth.

She sat up and found her clothing where he had tossed it. She dressed and went, moving through the house, its rooms in twilight, its decay masked. She felt at home there with the dust and the smell and the disuse. The St. Joseph had been small, plaster, the size of her hand, stolen from the nativity scene in the living room. Aurora had given it to her to hold while she dug. He wore a brown painted robe. He held a staff, the other arm extended, beckoning. He was the patron saint of the family and home, Aurora told her. That night was damp and starless. She had remembered to put on the quilted robe her mother gave her, draped across the foot of her bed.

"This is for the best," Aurora said as she dug. Nell had smelled licorice on her breath that came out, cloudlike, around her head. Aurora swore her to secrecy. She told Nell that her mother and Vince would be better apart. "Sometimes that is the way of things," she said. In her fervent child's heart Nell had wished it so.

It was Nell's mother who told Vince the statue was there, somewhere, who'd watched his drunken, desperate search from the doorway. Aurora packed and left the house in a cab. Nell, watching him on the lawn from her bedroom window, had felt her complicity. Vince dug for hours in the wrong place. He had made holes, they saw in the morning, all across the front lawn, cutting through the Saint Augustine with his trowel, scattering little clods of grass and dirt. A day later the buried statue would become part of her mother's and Vince's reconciliation, a joke between them, and in the living room the remaining figures in the nativity scene continued to pose in their tableau—Mary alone by the infant, her blue robe chipped, the wise man standing aside, waiting, his gift glued into his wonderful hands.

Nell stood on the lawn in the lamplight. She had forgotten her sweater, and the cold slipped down the front of her blouse. From the front porch she took twelve steps along the azaleas and stopped. The statue was there behind the hedge, buried close to the house. Nell moved in among the dry branches and scraped at the dirt with her hand. It was dense with the azalea roots, and smelled as she remembered it, of the fertilizer Vince used to make the shrubs bloom. Around her the neighborhood houses lit up warm and yellow. The darkness was a body bending over the hedges. She was not sure who watched her or if she was entirely alone. But she fell to her knees because she had once held the little statue in her hand, and she knew where to find it, prostrate in the bed of soil, its robe's folds the same, its plaster palm upturned, still held out in the semblance of redemption. And though Nell's limbs kept Teddy's memory fresh like a wound, she sensed, already, the unconscionable ease with which she would forget him.

breach

On our third day they find the boy's white dinghy upturned, scuttling back and forth in the breakers on the sandbar. It is midmorning. You are still sleeping. The beach is dotted with children excavating sand with their toes, gathering at the water's lapping edge to point and wonder. No one knows what the thing is until a man in a cottage further down rises with his coffee and binoculars and makes it out. He bangs on the cottage door next to ours and rouses the boy's father from last night's stupor. The father emerges in his madras shirt. I see his groggy look, his hand brushing back his hair. They head out with a neighbor in a motorized Sunfish and retrieve the dinghy. We all know the boat once they bring it in. We all think the same thing: the boy didn't pull it up high enough overnight when the tide came in. Some of us return to morning toast, the newspaper, the tending of small children, the breakfast dishes. I stay at my window, peering out.

The mother of the boy stands on her screened-in porch in her bathrobe, clutching the sash. I can just make out the tautness of her hands.

I hear her small cry, and I know she has checked the boy's bed and found it empty, that she waits now for something other than a boat drawn up onto the warming sand, three men wiping off their hands. I imagine decorum, disbelief, prevents her from running out onto the beach. She calls from behind the porch screen. "Where is he?" Her voice is tight and edged and merciless. The three men stop. Their hands fall, useless at their sides. Two of them look at each other. The third, the father, faces the woman behind the porch screen. On his face is the look of a man who wonders what she could possibly mean—exasperated, without patience.

In the room behind me you turn and the old bedsprings recoil.

"Come back to bed," you say. Your voice is full of the same annoyance I read on the father's face. The breeze is still damp and sweet. The foghorn that woke me has stopped its lament. The sun burns slowly through the haze, and I see the little pebbles, the iridescent pieces of shells, rolled and tumbled together at the water's edge. The yellowed window shade flaps.

"I don't want to," I say back. My body has cooled, separated from yours.

I hear you groan. We are vacationing on the Connecticut shore, in this cottage rented for three times what my family paid twenty years ago. A narrow, tarred street fronting a salt marsh accesses the cottages that stand all in a row on stilts, painted different colors. They are untidy and small, each distinct with the clutter of families with young children—brightly colored floats and tubes, tennis rackets and buckets and fishing poles thrown on porches, clotheslines sagging with towels and bathing suits. When we arrived, driving down the row of cottages to our own, I sensed your disappointed silence but pretended I didn't.

Outside, the moment of the men's idleness passes. They turn to each other and gather that they must take charge. On the beach are the charred remains of last night's bonfire and the tents the children made of the heavy woolen blankets provided with each cottage. One of the men ducks his head inside them, searching. The children by the water step toward each other, forming a small group. Men from other cottages come out. Their screen doors close on rusty springs, a loud bang followed by two softer ones. Nearly all of the men are fathers, some uncles, visiting for the weekend. They consult, hungover, unshaven. They inspect the dinghy—its fiberglass bottom scraped raw on broken shells and sand. There are holes big enough to put a finger through. Might he have rowed out too far, in fog, and the boat filled with water? Would he have tried to swim and lost his bearings? In one of the cottages a child begins to wail. The men on the beach disband with a seeming plan. Up and down the row of cottages I hear murmurs on the screened-in porches. I imagine the women whispering back and forth, their coffees' steam a willowy stem. Most are dressed by now in their bathing suits, some in shorts and halter tops, on their way out to the Laundromat at Black Hall or the A&P in Old Lyme. Today, the mothers abandon all plans. They call in the children, their voices conveying the sharp urgency that accompanies a reprimand. The water still laps, quiet as a clam.

When we arrived the cottage was the same as I remembered. Nothing had changed, not the kitchen linoleum, or the old countertops, the knotty pine walls, the burned-in outline of an iron dropped by a great-aunt, a child in 1945, on the floor by the nook cupboard. All of the cottages are the same. They hold the same tweedy upholstered couch and chair, the same desk and brass-armed lamp bolted to the wall, its shade a tobacco-colored map of old sea trade routes. The shelves of the nook cupboards are lined with dark green drinking glasses, faceted, like emeralds. In the kitchen cabinets, similar aluminum cookware, plastic plates and bowls and cups. As a child I'd visited the cottages of friends and been surprised by the sameness. Now, I am reassured. The past is partly recoverable, I thought. I told you this, and you shrugged, tossed your bag down at the bottom of the narrow stairwell. "No, it isn't," you said. Your hands, free of the bag, reached out to clasp the tops of my arms. You buried your expression in my hair.

It is July, warm enough not to need a fire, but the smell of wood smoke tells of mornings chilly with fog when my sisters and brother and I sat wrapped in blankets in front of the fireplace. Girls came around calling "Doughnuts" in plaintive voices, and we fished money from our sleeping parents' pockets to buy a dozen; glazed and cinnamon and chocolate iced. Once, I told you, I drove with the girls to the bakery in Sound View, where they loaded up the car's trunk with the white bakery boxes. Then, I walked up and down the row of cottages with them, carrying the boxes in my arms, my jean cuffs dragging and fraying in the wet sand, the fog encircling our ankles. When I told you this, it was our first morning here and we were still in bed. You had your hand spread flat on my stomach, your face pressed to my breast. I was twelve the summer I helped sell the doughnuts, my body sleek and still unwanted, like a boy's.

There is no television. Instead, we read all day long on the beach. We watch the tide come in and deposit long brown strands of kelp, Irish moss, and dead man's fingers. One day, the delicate remains of a horseshoe crab. You give nicknames to the people in the other cottages, invent their lives, critique their bodies in their swimsuits, and then head inside for long naps on the couch. I stay to listen to the families squabble. The fathers gather in the late afternoons with cans of beer or glasses iced and clinking, silent behind their sunglasses. The mothers sit in low-slung chairs by the water, dabbling feet, keeping an eye out. I try to hear what they are saying, what they talk about, but their voices and the shushing water meld. Some evenings, dressed in sundresses and pink skirts and floral blouses, the mothers head out with their husbands to dinner at the Griswold Inn, and I see the kind of clothing they wear in their regular lives—pretty and pleasing, mothers' costumes.

I watch the children with their buckets on the jetty, how they still, as I once did, crush the mussel shells with rocks and tie them to string, dangle the string into the jetty's crevices. The jetties are covered with snails and barnacles, slippery with algae. The mussels' meat is bright orange. The little ones shriek, afraid of the crabs they catch. One day, the boy who rows the white dinghy caught an eel and flung the abhorrent thing back. He rows out every day, his arms brown and strong.

"He reminds me of my brother in his boat," I told you the first time I saw him.

That day, he dragged the boat up on the sand and I had gone over to talk to him. He was eleven or twelve, with sun-bleached hair. He kept a distracted distance, born from shyness. I told him how I came to this same cottage as a child, that my brother had a boat like the dinghy. It was made of fiberglass, its interior a pale aqua color, with a place for a daggerboard and a mast and a rudder. They boy's face lit up. "This may be his boat, then," he said. He told me they found it across the street, abandoned behind the dilapidated shed. They'd had it repaired, he said. But they didn't outfit it with a sail.

"I remember the mast and sail leaning by the furnace in my parents' basement," I told him, laughing.

The father and another man have taken the Sunfish back out. I imagine there is hope of finding the boy elsewhere—clinging to a jetty, wandering the beach at Point O'Woods. The mother is dressed now, in wrinkled shorts and a T-shirt, and scrambling along the row of cottages, tapping on doors. "Is he here?" she asks, wondering if he has spent the night with friends. She does not come to our cottage. We are childless, just the two of us. During the long afternoons I've seen the looks we get from the husbands, from the wives. The women smile in our direction, covertly, almost wistfully, with masked envy. The men stare, bold and sniggering. Inside our cottage, at all times of the day, we have sex, exactly as they suspect. I have brought you here because this is the closest I could get to sleeping with you in my childhood bed. I had meant to show you something of my life, but my body is enough. You do not seem to need anything else.

I told you the story of the gypsies in the blueberries. I walked you down Center Avenue and showed you the place that was once a cart path, where my father as a boy used to walk to work in the afternoons. He held a job at One Hundred Acres Golf Course. The gypsies, he said, came each summer in wagons and stayed in the clearing, picking the wild blueberries. All of the children were instructed to keep away. The gypsies stole children, placed them in burlap sacks, flung them over their shoulders and ran down a secret path into the blueberry thicket. I think about this now, faced with the drama below me on the beach. I imagine the boy taken off in a painted wagon. I see him eyeing his captors, eating blueberries, almost happy to be off on an adventure. The gypsies were wild-haired and dark, my father said. He would pause to take a long sip of his watery drink. "Beware," he told us all, small children stunned by apprehension. The afternoon I told you this, you took my hand and tugged me into the long shed by the tiny beach store. Light came in through cracks in the plank walls. I made out the shapes of the old wooden rowboats we used to rent, the broken Adirondack chairs piled up in a stack. It smelled of freshly cut firewood and oil paint, of the dried leaves that had blown in and become part of the dirt floor. Once, there had been a swing hung from a great elm outside. As children we would come to the store for raspberry-flavored candy and *Archie* comics. Now, the elm leaves whirred with insects. You and I were in our bathing suits. Mine came off, quickly, efficiently, in your hands.

Now, I lean into the window frame, place my head on my folded arms. I think about going down to the beach to discover what is happening with the boy, but I realize I am watching the shape of the father in the Sunfish, his rumpled madras shirt, and waiting for him to return. I see the mother pass by our cottage. She stands by the water, hugging herself, watching the Sunfish crawl past the sandbar, beyond the jetty barrier, into the open current of the sound. Three children come down the beach to stand by her side, two little girls in one-piece suits, another older girl in a bikini, her legs long and thin. They do not touch the mother. They stand around her like sentries, casting up occasional looks. Under their feet they tread the delicate butter shells my grandmother taught me to string into bracelets.

Last night, there was a bonfire on the beach in front of the cottage next door. You and I watched, at first, from the screened-in porch. The husbands and wives circled the fire in their low-slung chairs. They had bottles of wine wedged down into the sand. Every so often someone offered to freshen drinks made in the dark green glasses. They knew we were there on the porch, and eventually the father of the boy in the white dinghy called up to us to join them. There was a kind of vocal flutter from the group—not quite laughter. You and I looked at each other, but you were up before I said anything, eager for the distraction. The screen door banged behind you. They made room for us in the circle. Someone gave up a chair for me, and you sat cross-legged on my right. The fire spit and blew sparks. The smoke burned my eyes. You urged me to tell my story of the gypsies, but I would not. Instead I told them how when I was young the mothers and fathers all sat in similar circles around fires on the same beach. Once, I said, the fathers all decided to row out to the motorboat buoyed beyond the jetty. It was my father's boat, and the idea was probably his. They took the boat out and the mothers sat abandoned around the fire, furious at first, then, as it grew later, more and more fearful.

I saw the faces in the circle glance out toward the dark water. None could imagine doing anything so foolish.

"But they came back," someone said, after a while.

"Oh yes," I tell them. "Eventually."

They had docked at a restaurant in Niantic and gone inside to the bar. How they made it back to the beach, the lone buoy glowing in the dark, none could say. Someone stood up in the little dinghy on the way in and it capsized, the mothers shrieking down by the water's edge wearing sweaters, clutching their drinks. The fathers returned to the fire, chastened, their clothing wet and steaming. I did not tell them how the children, left on the fringes of the bonfire, did what they wanted—sometimes even sitting undetected by a mother's elbow. I saw now that their own children were gathered on the beach, lining up the Adirondacks, draping them with blankets to make tents. We had even done that, once, and been bitten by sand fleas, woken up freezing, the blankets soaked from dampness and the tide that had risen to lick their woolen edges.

As a child, I had watched the fathers flip the dinghy that night through the same window from which I now watch the fathers search for the boy. Then, my sister and I shared the bed behind me. I had gasped with fear, and she had risen and come up to see what was wrong. She was my little sister, and I would not let her look. Now I see the men, joined by a dispatched Coast Guard boat, turn to head in. A group of mothers holding infants gathers on the water's rim. The older children, ordered to watch their siblings, sit bored in the growing heat near the cottages' wooden stilts, running the sand through their hands, telling little brothers and sisters to dig holes to China with bright plastic shovels. I see a man in his crisp police uniform, badge and buckle shining, emerge from between two cottages and head toward the group in leather shoes.

Last night at the bonfire the boy's father had leaned toward me and whispered something into my hair. His breath was warm with whiskey. I didn't hear what he said, so he leaned over again. He was smiling. "Take a walk with me," he said. I gave him a look of surprise and shook my head. After, his eyes were mournful, staring into the fire as if he was alone and had forgotten he'd spoken to me. I saw he was very drunk. I watched his profile in the firelight, sharp and handsome, and I felt something for him, a longing, a blooming need. For the three days of our stay I have watched him travel the jetty with his children, swinging the mussel shells tied to string. I've seen him launch the dingy with his son at the oars, giving it a gentle shove. I imagined he has seen me looking, that he's looked back at me with a tacit understanding, shaken his head at me, slowly, his mouth soft and tentative. *You and I know each other,* his look has said. *What is it you really want?* During the long afternoons I have felt his gaze. Once or twice, I have glanced over and met it. I have smiled at him, mildly. I have feigned indifference. Now, I see him wade into shore, tugging the Sunfish. I see him approach the police officer like a small child, beaten down by fear and guilt. His shoulders slope under his madras shirt. I imagine he smells, still, of whiskey, and his eyes carry the same mournful weight. Behind me you toss in the bed, throw off the blanket, smash the pillow. I hear your feet hit the floor and you are up, moving through the room.

"I can't take this," you say. You mean everything, but you pretend to mean the heat in the room. During the day it fills the upstairs, heavy and oppressive.

"Get up, then," I say.

You will go out on the beach with a newspaper, disgruntled about my avoiding you, and find out what is happening. If I stay at the window, I will hear our own porch door bang shut. You will pull one of the blankets off the Adirondacks and drag a chair to the front of our cottage to sit in, and notice that the children's tents block our view. I move from the window and open one of the pine dresser drawers. I take out a swimsuit and change; go down the sandy stairwell to the porch. Below me you yank the blankets off the chairs. The sand whips up, caught in the breeze. You throw the blankets in a heap. I watch your torso spin, your arms heave. I see your body suddenly different in its angry contortions. The neighbors have dispersed. The police officer nods, solemn and businesslike. I see the mother's eyes wide and hopeful, watching his face. I see the father put his hands in his hair and turn away to scour the horizon. When his hands drop they have their own texture and shape. I see them as beautifully wrought.

"What's all this?" you ask. You sit in one of the chairs, your head tipped back.

"They found the boy's boat out there this morning," I tell you through the screen.

"So he's missing," you say, finally.

"Yes. That's it," I say.

I am afraid to go onto the beach. My heart makes a small fluttering My limbs are weak. I want to go out and fold up the blankets and put them in a pile. I want to be helpful and ease everyone's fear, tell the mother and the father that the boy has gone to Sound View to play the games in the arcade. He is there, buying fried dough with money he stole from the top of your bureau. He has gone out onto the salt marsh, followed the little path my sisters and brother and I made years ago. He is hiding out and simply waiting to appear.

I stand on my porch and the father looks up and sees me. On his face is an awful complicity.

"Make some coffee," you call up from the beach.

I am relieved and saddened to have a reason to turn away. In the kitchen I can view the road and the police officer's car. I see the children perched on the low brick walls, whispering. Beyond them the haze burns off the salt marsh. It is a hot, humid day. The breeze has died out. I make coffee and notice my hands trembling. Last night around the fire I had too much to drink. The night became blurred—part fire, part sand and wind. The faces of the mothers and fathers slid and shifted. The little waves came in. Beyond the bonfire the beach was dark. I got up to go inside. I remember I got up and walked off. Somehow, I missed the steps to our porch. I see that now, that I climbed the wrong set of steps and went into the wrong cottage. I was inside, stumbling through the kitchen to the bathroom. And he was there, the father. I wonder now if he had leaned over again while we sat by the fire and asked me to meet him. The kitchen was dark. The porch light was a yellow bulb swarmed by moths. We stood there, looking at each other.

I stand in my own kitchen now and feel the tender bruises on my body from the days of sex with you—on my elbows, the insides of my thighs, the ridges of my spine, and yet last night I could have taken him in my arms. He would fit there, as if our bodies had planned it. I would feel his warm chest under the madras shirt. His mouth would be desperate and greedy, his chin gritty with stubble. His sighs would make my heart swim. I see how it might have been if I hadn't laughed, awkwardly, and stepped away from him, declaring my mistake. I went out the backdoor facing the road and walked to our cottage, and he stood behind the screen, watching me. I walked slowly, glancing over my shoulder at him, willing him to find the words to call me back, but he did not. In our own kitchen, everything was the same—the bathroom door ajar, the smell of soap and shampoo, the open kitchen shelves of canned and packaged food. The only difference was the air, its silence and shadow unmarked by the charge of our bodies. I returned to my chair by the bonfire on the beach.

"You went in the wrong cottage," you said. You looked at me, carefully. You held an empty green glass, shot through with orange sparks.

"I know," I said. "I made a mistake."

And I saw you did not believe me. I felt my body, bright and alive in the firelight. I saw the boy's father step from the darkness and circle the chairs.

"Here's Carson," one of the men said.

"Where are the drinks?" another asked. There was general laughter all around. Carson slipped into the chair beside me. He smelled familiar, like an old shirt. His hands were empty, resting on his knees. Everything around me grew keen and sharp—the little waves moving up the beach, the fire's sputter, its whitened logs, the aluminum legs of the chairs, the empty glasses half-buried beside them. Carson's wife eyed me in her quiet, wistful way. You stood to leave and I felt it then, the dull, inevitable withdrawing.

Now, I bring you coffee in one of the cottage's old turquoise mugs. The beach is empty, the sand warm. Everything has changed, yet the day proceeds quietly. The white dinghy stays upturned in the high, dry sand by the cottage. Someone brings an oar, washed up further down the beach. Someone else appears with a red tackle box, the bobbins and hooks, the saltwater lures, all lost from their plastic compartments. These items sit beside the boat like assembled relics. Under the porch steps is a bucket of crabs in water. Their bodies still move, hesitantly, the claws scraping against the bucket's plastic sides. We all wait for news of the boy. Families come out of the cottages and gather in small, hushed groups. By late afternoon the children are allowed to display their heedlessness. They dive from the jetty and make flotillas with the colored rafts. The boy's family stays inside. In our proximity we hear their shouting, its tones of anguish and accusation.

Eventually, you go inside and expect me to follow you, but I will not. I watch the Coast Guard boat comb the sound. I watch the sun brighten the rim of Long Island. I hear the drawers of the pine bureau scrape open and bang shut, signs that you are packing to leave. I do not stop you. I cannot raise myself from the wooden chair, from my vigil. I scan the water's edge, waiting for more debris to wash in, for the boy's body, tumbled and softened, delivered to his parents' door in a wash of foam and seaweed. And then someone lights a grill for dinner, and the smell of cooking comes from underneath the cottages, and you stand on the porch clearing your throat.

"Well, I'm going," you say.

I have just awoken in the Adirondack chair. I have dreamed of swimming in churning water and tasting salt. I am out of sorts, my hair damp and tangled, my chest tight, as if I have been holding my breath.

"I'm wondering," I say. "If he didn't go out there, to the mouth of the sound. It's a place called the Race. When the tides change water rushes through breaches, and there are rip currents."

It is evening, and the breeze is back, cooler, roughened with sand.

"They catch bluefish there," I tell you. I hear you sigh.

"So, that's it, then," you say.

The breeze shifts and twists. Sand forms small spouts. I need to change from my suit into warmer clothes. I realize this concern for myself is not normal in the middle of all this—you on the porch with your bag packed, the family next door with a boy lost. Still, I find nothing to say to stop you. You will not listen to any more stories, and my body is tired, dulled from its use as a lure. I hear your footsteps cross the porch and recede into the house. I think I hear the back screen door close, the sound of the cab you must have called pulling away. I feel the cottage behind me, its familiar rooms ringing with your absence.

For two long days, I languish. I see Carson on the shadowy porch. I see him out on the beach in the dark, the sparks flying from his cigarette's lit end, his shirttails waving. Overhead the moon is a worn shell. I pass him on my walk to the little store, and he is irretrievable, like his son. The weather stays warm and sunny, undaunted by tragedy. The mussel shards glitter in their piles on the beach. The water thickens with seaweed like soup. I witness the family's reluctance to accept the truth. One day they enlist us all to search the salt marsh. We follow sandy paths along channel-fed branches, fight blackflies in the neck-high grass, and return, our clothing damp with sweat. The next night the search party members split up and head in opposite directions down the beach, calling the boy's name. I want to tell them that he has moved beyond the reach of the longing in their voices. I imagine him, his brown arms and bright hair, bumping along in a gypsy wagon on a cart path toward New Haven.

And then, on the third dazzling afternoon, the air salty and rank with mussels and seaweed, the family next door packs their Suburban, loads it with duffel bags, ties the bikes up on the roof's rack. They leave behind their floats, tucked under the cottage, and the dinghy, its white hull upturned on the beach. The older girl tends to the young ones, her arms around each shoulder. The other children seem blanched, despite their tans. The mother moves mechanically in her pretty clothes. At last Carson, grim and unapproachable, slips behind the wheel. He will drive down the narrow, tar road and cease to be the man who faced me in his cottage kitchen. I see us all, in the space of our lives, as pieces in constant alteration, revolving and joining, clashing and missing. You must understand it was never about sex. It was always what I see now in the mother's face, what surfaces, buoyant and relentless, in the body's absence.

beautiful

She was just Lorna when she applied for the job. She wore bangs and cutoff jean shorts and flip-flops. She went with her new friend, Yolie, who was already a bartender there, her exposed skin sticking to the seat of Yolie's car in the Florida heat. Yolie told Lorna he would like her, not to worry, and pulled her through the door into the darkness of the club. The expanse of it was empty and wide and dank, the oval shaped bar was lit underneath by yellow bulbs up on a dais in the center of the room, and all around were sections with booths cordoned off by brass railings. He came out from the office in the back. His eyes in the dark held a phosphorescence. His shirt was a blue oxford, untucked. He wore leather slippers.

"Arlo," Yolie said. He seemed as if he would walk past them, jingling his ring of keys.

"Oh," he said. He stopped and Yolie put her arms around his neck and kissed his unshaven cheek.

"This is Lorna," she said. He looked over at her, and she heard him breathe, one breath in, then out. The keys in his hand shook.

"Yes," he said. He looked down at the keys.

They followed him back to the door into the office. Inside, under garish fluorescent light, sat a glass-topped desk and a leather armchair behind it, and on the floor dingy, gold sculptured carpet. The walls were paneled, the kind people put in their 1970s refinished basements. A full-length mirror leaned against one wall, near a door that led into a small, white-tiled bathroom. He took a leotard from its wire hanger and handed it to her.

"You'll have to try this on," he said, looking at the shimmering thing held in the air between them. He appeared hesitant, almost apologetic. When she took the leotard from his hand their fingers touched, and she stared at his face, pale and damp under the new beard, waiting for him to look up, but he did not. Yolie pushed her, grinning, into the bathroom, and shut the door. In the dim bathroom light she was alone, and her heart raced. The leotard, red with white stripes on the bottom, blue on top with white stars, looked like a Wonder Woman costume. She moved quickly, taking off her clothes. She could not wear anything under the leotard because of the high cut on the legs, the scoop at the neck and back.

"You need to come out," Yolie said.

She did not want to leave the bathroom with its dull light. In the mirror over the sink she saw her flushed cheeks, the sheen of sweat along the top of her breasts. She saw her chest rise and fall with her own frightened breath. But she needed the job, and it didn't matter, she told herself, what anyone thought. So she opened the door and stepped barefoot onto the gold carpet, into the spotlight of overhead fluorescence. He looked at her body in the leotard, but not her face. He stared at her so long she looked down at herself. "What?" she asked, masking her embarrassment with anger. And then he looked up into her eyes, his own eyes creased and pained.

"You are beautiful," he said, quietly. The way he said it made it something she believed for the first time in her life.

Months later, the club closes and reopens under new ownership as a country and western saloon. One night, Lorna is on the back of a boy's motorcycle, riding very fast on a major thoroughfare, and the streetlights and the headlights of cars and the storefronts in the strip malls and the white lines on the road all seem bright smears. It is early spring, the air sharp, carrying the smell of exhaust and the perfume of women in cars with the windows rolled down, and further off, orange groves in bloom. She holds the boy tightly around his waist, feels his stomach muscles under his thin T-shirt, presses herself up against his back, and she both wants and fears the speed at which they travel, believing, because he has told her he loves her, that he will not do anything to harm her. He slows down in front of a strip mall and pulls into an empty parking lot and tells her to get off.

"Come on," he says, as if time is pressing. It is late at night and no one is around.

"Tell me you love me," he says. Lorna looks at him, his hair blown back, his soft, brown eyes, the chin with the cleft.

"You know I do," she says. His face reflects a dawning despair. He takes off on the motorcycle without her and rides headlong toward a stucco wall at the end of the lot, and does not slow down or attempt to stop until the last moment, when he applies the brake and slides to the side. He rights the bike and heads back to where she stands, with her hands over her face.

"Were you watching?" he asks.

"What are you doing?" she wants to know.

"Tell me you love me," he says again, and he gives the bike some gas and the back wheel spins on the black tar lot. And she hesitates because suddenly she doubts her love for him at the moment that she must not, and he sees and accelerates toward the wall, his speed even greater this time, the sound of the engine rising at an increasingly higher pitch, until she finds her breath stopped in her chest. But he pulls back like before, at the last minute. He rides back to her, and looks up at her, tears streaking his face.

"I love you," she says, and he tells her to get back on the bike, and she does, her arms around his waist shaking with something she will never identify for sure. Fear? Love? Desire? Or are they all, she wonders, the same?

At first, Lorna worked afternoons at Arlo's club to learn the job. But it was so slow she didn't learn much. There was always someone else with her to show her things:

"This is the soda gun, for ginger ale and club soda and all," each small button's code long eroded. "You just remember, you know, top is Coke, left is soda, right is ginger ale." That was Susie, who set her long blond hair in electric rollers so that it bounced and swung around when she moved, wiping out ashtrays, restacking glasses, checking the stock in the beer cooler. She spoke quickly in a high-pitched voice, her blue eyes darting up and down the bar, watching the only three customers. "This is the well, you know, it goes vodka, gin, rum, bourbon, tequila, and then the grenadine and the triple sec." Lorna nodded at everything, and promptly forgot it afterward.

"Why don't you go see if that guy wants another one," Susie said. She lit a cigarette. Lorna dreaded confronting the man. She wasn't used to herself in the leotard, the required L'eggs Sheer Energy suntan pantyhose, the high-heeled shoes. She had taken on a role she could not perform. Susie gave her a look. *Go,* it said.

Lorna walked down the length of the bar and stood in front of the customer. He wore a golf shirt and his thinning blond hair swiped to one side. The sun had freckled the bridge of his nose. The skin around his eyes was puffy and white where his sunglasses sat.

"I've been waiting for you to come over," he said, under his breath.

She didn't know what to do with her hands so she placed them on the edge of the wooden bar. She smiled, but his eyes, moving from her face to the blue-backed stars on her chest, unnerved her, and she felt the smile falter, and knew he saw.

"Would you like another drink?" she asked.

"If *you* bring it to me," he said, and put the glass to his wet lips and tipped his head all the way back to drain it. He placed it back on the bar and the ice resettled. "I'm drinking rye," he told her. She took the glass in her hand and he put his hand on hers to stop her. His hand was heavy and cold, and he gripped hers tightly, so she could not walk away. "I'm not going to even ask your name," he said, his eyes intent. "I just know you know what we would be like together. And I'm going to give you this card," and he pulled a white business card out of his shirt pocket, "and I want you to call me." He placed the card on the top of the bar. Lorna looked down at it, and the customer still held her hand. "Take it," he said, his voice low, melodious, laced with threat, and she picked it up with her free hand, and he let her go.

Lorna had no idea what making the drink entailed. She looked at the liquor bottles on their mirrored shelves, reading all of the labels. Susie watched her. "Rye," she said, annoyed. When Lorna could not find the bottle, and glanced up at her in defeat, Susie grabbed one from a top shelf and made her the drink.

"You be nice to that girl, Susie," the customer called from the end of the bar. "I like this one."

Susie handed the drink to Lorna. She smiled, showing all her teeth. She flounced her hair. Lorna brought the man the drink and placed it on a white napkin in front of him, enduring his stare, his wet grin. She took the ten he handed her, his fingers lingering on the bill, along her palm. She couldn't remember the price of the drinks. They hadn't let her do the money yet, so she gave the bill to Susie.

"The rest of that is for you," the customer yelled. "And Susie-Q, her ass is sweeter than yours."

None of this mattered, Susie said. They pooled their tips. Lorna worked two afternoons with Susie, and didn't see Arlo at all. There was another man there, Larry, Arlo's assistant. He would lean on the bar and smoke cigarettes and ask her questions about herself.

"Where are you from?" he would ask, and Lorna would pretend to be busy, wiping the top of the bar with a damp rag. "And you left because . . . ? " She would lift his cigarette out of the red plastic ashtray and dump the butts, then replace the cigarette and set the whole thing back in front of him.

"Because I wanted to," she told him.

"Do you always do what you want to do?" he asked her. He had a wide mouth and dark eyes that were always only half serious. She looked at him, and he blew his cigarette smoke out of his nose. "I mean, look, Lor, it's really slow in here, and we're both doing nothing, so what do you want to do *right now*?" he asked, the words carrying a significance she would pretend not to understand.

On the third afternoon Lorna worked with Yolie, and both Larry and Arlo came into the bar. Arlo wore his usual shirt unbuttoned halfway down his chest as if he'd forgotten to finish dressing. His hair looked dirty. He shuffled past the bar without acknowledging her and approached Larry.

"Who the fuck is that?" he asked.

Larry looked up at Lorna with mild surprise.

Afterward, Yolie laughed, reassuring her. "That afternoon he hired you he was out of his mind," she said. "You're just lucky."

Arlo came out of the office later and stopped at the bar. He was slight and almost delicate, like a boy, but older than the boys Lorna knew. His hair hung in wisps over his eyes. He always held a cigarette. Sometimes his hand shook, other times it didn't. On this afternoon he stood in near darkness and watched her bring a drink to a customer. With his eyes on her now, Lorna felt awkward, hideous. He whistled under his breath. "Oh baby," he said. "You have amazing legs." She wanted to turn on him and strike him. She wanted to take his face in her hands and kiss his mouth.

After the country and western saloon closes, the club becomes a Chinese buffet. Lorna works as a hostess at the airport's revolving rooftop restaurant. She wears a long, black Lycra skirt and seats elaborately dressed couples on their anniversaries, businessmen in dark suits, their hair cut cleanly around their ears. She loses track of the tables as the restaurant turns, spills Tom Collinses onto a woman's silk lap. But she meets a man who calls her "Lo" and takes her out in his Ferrari. They eat outside at an iron table on the leafy patio of a famous hotel restaurant on the beach, and he pours her wine and lights her cigarettes and they talk. They watch the sunset, which strikes her as overly pink and orange. She tells him how different the beaches are where she grew up, and he asks the differences, his head cocked to one side, his eyes warm and interested. She explains the ones she can articulate—the sand on the beach is coarse and brown, and the water is darker, and colder, more green. She is not able to tell how the debris that washes up, the pieces of trees, the milk cartons, the occasional shoe, makes the beach feel like suffering. But he intuits a kind of sadness in the way she describes it and looks at her with compassion. He has graying hair and a wry smile that she likes because it reminds her of someone else. At the end of the night he tells her she has a beautiful heart, but there is only that one weekend in a room in the pink hotel on soft, expensive sheets, and then he will not see her again.

When she got the job at Arlo's club, Lorna lived in an apartment complex with a pool surrounded by a hibiscus hedge, which for her was its most alluring feature. She shared an apartment with a girl she met some weeks before, temping at an insurance company, and spent her free afternoons lying out in the sun by the red flowers and the chlorinated blue pool water. Here, dragonflies dipped and circled her body on the chaise, their wings opaque and gold-veined, their hovering movements timed, it seemed, to inaudible music. She slit her eyes against the sun and watched them, their appearance in a multitude like a portent. She dreamed about Arlo, how she might kiss his smooth chest, the softness above the button of his pants, how his mouth would slide into his smile, one side first, tentatively, fearful of revealing too much.

She had already forgotten her boyfriend, who had brought her to Florida, run out of money, and gone back up north without her. She told him to go because his only skill was as a painter, and it was too hot, he whined, to paint here, and anyway, she did not love him, and did not want to support him. The only problem with his leaving was that now she had no car. Her roommate was never home, so Lorna could not ask her for rides. One day, Yolie picked her up for work at the club, but the other days she asked a neighbor to drive her. She had seen him in the afternoons at the pool, pretending not to watch her climbing out of the water. She saw him leave the complex at night in a silver Fiat, the top down, his hair slicked back with gel. When she approached him at the pool about the ride, he was lying on a striped towel on a chaise, his torso oily, smelling of coconuts. He stared at her bare stomach, considering, then back up to her face. He grinned.

"Well, sure," he said. He drove her, willingly, almost joyfully, his hand sliding on the stick shift, his legs revealed in shorts, covered with curly hair. He would shave and put on a pressed shirt before he picked her up, and she realized, with an almost faraway kind of acceptance, that she would owe him in some way. One day he would exact a price.

This happened when Arlo decided to close in the afternoons, and no one called her to let her know. She arrived at the club in the Fiat with the neighbor, and he slid his hand between her damp thighs and leaned over and kissed her. She turned away, but his mouth moved into her hair, and in her confusion and surprise she sprang from the car and slammed the door and stalked off. The Fiat sent up gravel at the parking lot exit before she realized the club was closed. From there she walked to the 7-Eleven in her high heels and suntan hose and cut off shorts, the leotard hot and clinging underneath. She called her roommate from the pay phone, knowing she was not home. She called Yolie and left a message. She wasn't able to think of anyone else. The manager of the store came out twice and asked her to move on. And then a car pulled in, a black 280Z. The boy ambled into the store in gym shorts, the back of his T-shirt wet with sweat, and came out, tapping his pack of cigarettes onto the palm of his hand. He made a sad face at her, one she accepted as sincere. And she thought, *This is OK, to be pitied.*

"Need a ride somewhere?" he asked.

And she gratefully got into the car.

The upholstery was slippery and cool. She told him the name of the apartment complex, which was all the way across town, a route that she had never paid attention to as a passenger. He took the interstate, humming to himself, and everything suddenly looked unfamiliar. She had never seen those houses with the tin roofs before.

"Which way are you going?" she asked. He looked at her, and shrugged.

"The only way I know," he said.

His cheeks were chubby. His mouth was small, the lips pursed. He was whistling, tapping his fingers on the steering wheel. He smelled of scented deodorant. He asked her name and she told him, "Lorna," but he didn't hear or didn't listen.

"Do you work at the club back there, Laura?" he asked. Her heart pounded in a place at the base of her neck. She put her hand on the door handle and imagined leaning on the door, jumping out onto the swiftly passing shoulder. She was sorry she slammed the neighbor's car door. She was sorry she didn't allow his kiss, his groping between her legs, as payment for the week's worth of rides. She wanted the air-conditioned darkness of the club. She craved Arlo's face, pictured it like a salve, the dry edges of his lips, his sorrowful brows, the reddened rim of his nose. She was sure she would never see him again.

She was sure she would suffer now, at the hands of this stranger whose car maneuvered skillfully at high speed between lanes of an interstate she did not know.

And then, "Here we go," the boy said, and they pulled into the complex with its withered tropical plants, its asphalt radiating heat. He gave her a piece of paper with his name and his phone number. She took it from him with a trembling hand, her eyes wet with unshed tears. "You really are pretty," he told her. And she recognized his pity again, his genuine sadness mixed with checked lust, and despised herself.

As the Chinese buffet, the building that once housed Arlo's club finally achieves some success. People flock there from the surrounding office complexes for inexpensive lunches. Lorna goes with some coworkers from Suncoast Realty one afternoon, and she does not realize it is the same place until one of the men mentions the outfits the bartenders wore there when it was a club, and another one recalls a night when he got into a fight in the parking lot. The two women shake their heads and roll their eyes, and Lorna looks around the interior of the restaurant and makes out the old brass railings, sees where the bar has been replaced with a sushi bar in the center of the room. She recognizes the same air-conditioned darkness. She foolishly admits she worked there, and the women raise their eyebrows and glance down into their plates, and the men stop chewing their food and never look at her the same way again. "Really?" one asks. They have trouble believing she served drinks when she is so inept at the copier and the coffeemaker, and though everyone laughs, a new tension invades their group, one that prevents the wave of memory from suffusing her. They nervously stack the white plates with the remains of rice and lo mein, gather their purses and pull out their wallets, preparing to leave. Later, the men begin to ask her out, and she refuses them, even the ones she has dreamed about alone at night, because she does not trust their attention, their eagerness to have her in their possession. Suddenly, the only thing she has that they desire isn't the thing she desires to give.

The leotards had been Arlo's last ploy to draw customers, but business was slowing down for good. There was still money on weekend nights, when a band came in and played on the stage up front, and people filled the tables in the sections beyond the brass rails and their bodies moved together on the dance floor, lined ten deep at the oval bar. Larry told Lorna that Arlo wanted her to work Friday and Saturday nights. She could make a rum and Coke and a Jack and Coke, a seabreeze and a screwdriver. Yolie showed her how to make a vodka martini. "That should be good enough," she said.

The first night she stumbled around behind the bar, in everyone's way. Six girls worked, three on each side, all of them with weighty hair and whip-thin legs, their leotards crawling up in back like thongs. Lorna acquired a reflexive motion of tugging hers down that customers found beguiling. She thrilled them in her idiocy.

"I'd like a kamikaze," someone might say, and she would look at them,

"And that is . . . ? " and the customer would throw his head back and laugh. Yolie, working next to her, would place her lips near her ear:

"Vodka, splash triple sec, splash lime." The bottles still felt heavy and slippery in her hand. She still pushed the wrong button on the gun. She miscounted change in her hurry to get out of the drawer. But by Saturday night she became used to approaching the people at the bar, their faces part of a larger blur that was the rest of the club, the band on the stage, the hum of bodies pressed in close. She liked the makeup she wore, her glossed lips, the way whatever she did, filling glasses with ice, tipping a bottle and replacing it in the well, bringing a drink to a customer, became timed to the band's music, her body its own song. She took the money the customers pushed toward her across the bar or folded into the palm of her hand, their eyes teasing and sly. She sensed the bargaining going on, none of it having much to do with the drinks. They paid, and they waited, and they never got what they wanted. Behind the bar, she was untouchable, on show, like a museum piece.

She aroused the fury of the other bartenders. They looked over at Arlo where he sat at the bar, wondering when he would notice her incompetence. But he said nothing, continued to sit and sip his drink, his eyes glassy and electric, following her movements. Now, Lorna wanted his eyes on her. She leaned over the bar and lit his cigarettes, and he gave her his slow-motion smile. He chatted with customers, ignoring the running of the club, the band's lengthy breaks, the scuffle erupting on the dance floor, Larry's pleas to return to the office and speak with someone on the phone. Arlo's eyes, watching her, felt like a caress.

At the end of the night he called her into the office. He sat under the fluorescent light in his leather chair counting out one of the register drawers. Larry was there with his half serious expression. Arlo had the drawers stacked on the floor and lines of cocaine on the glass top of the desk. He told Larry to get Lorna a drink, and Larry looked at her, smirking, and asked, "So, do you know what you want?" She stared at the top of Arlo's bent head, waiting for him to finish the line. When he looked up his eyes were watering and red.

"What should I drink?" she asked. She sat in a chair across from him, her legs curled up underneath her, her tips in the blue Crown Royal bag beside her on the floor. She played with her hair, piling it up on top of her head and letting it fall.

"Grand Marnier," he said. He settled back into his chair and they looked at each other. She did not know what he saw when he looked at her, but when he did something in his face broke and smoothed out, some slackening of disdain, a softness he didn't offer anyone else. She sipped the drink that Larry brought her in a tiny glass. It burned her throat, tasted of oranges, and deep down, an amber-tinted sadness. Arlo said nothing to her at all. The drawers stayed there stacked on the gold carpet, and he leaned back in his chair and tipped his head and watched her. She memorized his face, the shape of his hands, the soft hair on his arms below his rolled-up sleeves. He put his hand over his mouth, and they stared at each other endlessly, until Larry began to count the drawers, muttering to himself, and Yolie came in and told her she was ready to go home.

Eventually, even the Chinese buffet fails, and the club becomes an empty building with a for sale sign and weeds growing up through the parking lot. Lorna marries a man who makes the claim that he loves everything about her—her intelligence, her humor, the smell of her skin, because he knows this is what she wants to hear. She learns the truth when she discovers her role involves clothing and hairstyles and, among his friends, a certain silence. He becomes immune to what he saw as her beauty when she allows gray to thread her hair and lets her body lose its firmness, when too much dreaming pulls down the corners of her mouth. They live in a new subdivision where the houses are different but oddly the same, stucco homes painted in the hues of pastel Easter eggs. There is her own pool, with a screened enclosure, and beyond that a pond with water spraying up out of a fountain at the center. There are woods that she sees in the distance, and other neighbors with young children in strollers and leashed dogs, their porches and front lawns decorated for each holiday. She conceives two children but never carries them. She has an affair with a man, simple and straightforward, with no pretending he wants her for anything more than the one thing she has learned to give, expertly, with no trace of herself. She meets him at his apartment on his lunch hour, and when they are in bed together he asks her if she is happy. "What is happy?" she says. "What you pretend when you have everything you thought you wanted?" He turns his head on his pillow, decidedly miserable, and tells her he shouldn't see her anymore. And then one afternoon she comes out into her suburban yard and finds the dragonflies again, their dance among the one tree's branches and the bird-of-paradise. They have not meant anything until that moment, their power to foretell delayed by years.

She did not go home with Yolie that night. Larry counted the drawers and put money in zippered bank bags for the deposit. He stood in the doorway to the office, terse and concerned, for once completely serious. "You all set?" he asked Arlo. Arlo's head seemed heavy, his eyelids weighted. He waved Larry away with his hand. Larry made a noise under his breath and turned and left.

"You know why you're here?" Arlo asked her.

She had finished her drink and all the dark lines on the paneled walls wavered.

She stood up and crossed the gold carpet, knelt down in front of him in his leather swivel chair and put her hands on the tops of his legs. His brows knit together. He pulled back and took her hands in his. "Don't do this to me," he said. He shook his head and laughed, softly, the laugh catching in his throat. He looked away from her so she could not see his eyes. "I have nothing to offer you, sweetheart," he said.

She kissed him anyway, and he put his hands along her face, and Lorna slipped the leotard off her shoulders, each arm pulled from its sleeve, the outline of her bathing suit marked by her tan, the string ties, the cups of white. How she looked, loving him, her eyes shining with it, her mouth trembling on his, and then his mouth, wet and roaming, his hands on her shoulders shaking with the tremors of what he used to know as desire, the memory of it stirring in his head and nowhere else. He told her he wasn't worth it. He begged her to stop, and then said not to. He wished he could be who she wanted. She told him she loved him the way he was. But nothing she said or did was any use. His body, drained and wasted, refused them, and none of it, he assured her after they had tried and tried in the cold, air-conditioned office, was her fault.

His eyes took her in. "You are something," he whispered, sorry and sickened, his hands damp with regret along the side of her face.

"Just forget this," he told her. "Forget everything I said."

But watching the dragonflies she remembers. She sees how he must have called her into the office that night to let her go, how Larry had to do it the next day, telling her on the phone that they were cutting back, business was too slow. She recognizes her grief, the taste of oranges and bitterness mixed with his saliva in her mouth, all of it, in her confusion then, a betrayal. Now, standing in her front yard by the blooming plumbago, she can read Arlo's tortured eyes, feel his skin under her fingertips, hear his hoarse pleas against her neck, in her hair, and see how she has spent a long time foolishly searching for him in the faces of others. How could she have realized it was her love, expended that night, breathed out into the shoddy office, worn down under the fluorescent lighting, that would emerge flailing and beating, the most beautiful thing she has ever known?

apparitions

I saw Auntie Sister in my grandmother's barn when I was five. She sat in her black habit on a bale of hay in a shaft of sunlight. I waited nearby for her to notice me. Once, she had come to my house and sat on our front steps, her eyes full of laughter. Pieces of her dark hair snuck out of her wimple. She gave me a white leather-covered missal with gilt-edged pages, a silk ribbon bookmark, and colored illustrations—Jesus in all of them, a golden half-moon floating over his head. In the barn she sat still, imperturbable, and did not turn to greet me. I felt the cold of the damp stone floor. I felt I had interrupted something. I ran outside to where my mother and grandmother sat in garden chairs by a border of crocuses. Behind them the house's long porch trim had lacey cut-outs. The driveway shimmered, tiny white pebbles. I didn't tell them what I had seen. Much later, I learned that Auntie Sister, my grandmother's only sister, died in a car wreck on the Massachusetts Turnpike the year before I saw her, or didn't see her, sitting in the sunlight in the barn.

I thought of Auntie Sister as I stood at my window watching the black-haired teenage boy walk past my house. It was his fourth time by. His hair hung long and fine to his shoulders. He kept his eyes on his toes and placed his feet carefully down onto the pavement. Once in a while he stumbled. The shirt he had on could have been his father's, the kind of sport shirt worn by men who carry a cigar in their breast pocket, or tickets to a game. Over the shirt he wore a too-large navy blazer. It was a cold, gray morning that looked impossibly like snow. The smell of jasmine came through the open window. My acacia tree bloomed the yellow of Northeastern spring forsythia. I remembered the chill of the barn floor again, and felt that the boy, like Auntie Sister, was someone I shouldn't have been seeing, that I was the only one privileged to witness his passing.

It had been a month since my daughter took back her three-year old son, Nicholas. He had been mine for a year while she spent time in rehab and found a job and purchased a car, all things done under the guidance of a social worker. She had not ever wanted to listen to me. There were years of resentment between us—prompted by my divorcing her father. She did not trust or believe me. I might say that she did not love me, but it is childish to admit such things, even to yourself. Assume that love exists. She did not want me to have Nicholas, but there was no one else, so she was persuaded by the social worker to relent. Nicholas was born blind. He came to me with a little white cane, tapping it in my doorway. He held his two hands out and the social worker told me to kneel down. I knelt onto the kitchen's worn linoleum. I smelled his breath, cloying and sweet. He placed his small hands on my face.

"This is how he knows you," the social worker said. Her name was Renee, and she ran her own veined hand through her hair and dropped her folder of paperwork on my kitchen table. She sighed and asked me for coffee. Her eyes were creased, brimming with sad acceptance, and I would learn to trust her enough to eventually, at the end of a year, give him up. I measured time this way now, in relationship to this event. So when the teenager walked past my house, I marked it as a month plus a day that Nicholas had been gone. I had the windows open, and the cold air came through the room. Early spring is the only time Florida reminds me of New England. The humidity hasn't settled in. The temperature is unpredictable, and there is often a breeze. Everyone's yard holds some unexpected, tender bloom, and the trees brighten with the shoots of leaves. I live in a neighborhood of bungalows built in the 1940s. Our houses, cement block or wood, with metal awnings, are all in a modest state of disrepair. Most of my neighbors are old people, but there are some young families moving in. I am neither young nor old. I am just alone, which is justification to live here. We are all seemingly lonely. We walk the grid of neighborhood streets with dogs on leashes or singly in our windbreakers. The young mothers push their strollers. Even their lives seem tiresome and routine. Their faces show resignation. They are pale and slightly overweight. Their great diamond engagement rings flash from their fingers. At their houses they have expensive cars waiting for them in the driveways. And still, they recognize that they are bound to their children and their life in a way they hadn't expected. The burden pulls them down and subdues them and they cannot see beyond it.

It was never this way with Nicholas, though at first, I did not especially want him to live with me. I had agreed out of a sense of guilt for having failed my daughter. I blamed myself, but now I see I was the bandage she undid by leaving. I didn't know if I was capable of caring for her son. I was set in my own routine. I didn't own a television and sometimes I drank too much. I told this to Renee when she first called me.

"How much is too much?" she asked me.

"I wake up the next morning and my dishes are washed and put away, and I don't remember doing it," I told her.

I heard her scoff. "Do you wake up in your own bed?" she asked me.

"Of course," I said.

"Too bad," she said, and laughed. I laughed, too.

The day she brought Nicholas over we poured shots of Johnnie Walker into our coffees. We looked at each other across the vinyl tablecloth and I saw that she understood me.

"You don't know what will come of this," she said. "Maybe something unbelievably trying, maybe something amazing." I have learned there are people with a certain wisdom let loose in the world. Like milkweed, they are aloft and drifting. Once in a while they land into your open palm. Other times, sensing them, you must situate yourself in their path.

I watched the teenager pass my house for the fifth time. I opened my front door and went down the cement walk just as he turned the corner to the next block. He stopped then, with his back toward me, and bent down to scoop up something in the grass by the curb. The blazer and the shirt rode up his back. His pants were low on his hips. His back was thin, and I could see the ridges of his spine.

I remembered then the town picnic at the LaSalette Novitiate when I was fifteen. The Novitiate had been vacant for a long time, a large three-story brick structure built in 1904 with added ells, acres of woods, and meadows the Brothers of LaSalette used to farm. The picnic was given by the town's historical society as an attempt to raise funds and interest in the renovation of the building. I went to the picnic with my friend, Celia. We cut through the fields behind my house to get there. We brought a bottle of wine I took from a cupboard filled with bottles I was sure my parents would never miss. I remember the label now, a Chateau Latour 1947, an expensive one they would allude to, perplexed, for years. It was Indian summer, and the fields smelled of dried grass and withered leaves and goldenrod. We sat in the tall grass and drank. I had befriended Celia for her knowledge of sex, her talk about boys' mouths and hands and what they might do with them. We lay back in the grass so that only the sky with its reeling birds was visible. Celia's voice had a little ringing to it, like small bells. The order of LaSalette was founded on the apparition of Mary, and I knew the story and told it to her, how Mary appeared, weeping, to two children in the French Alps. The children had been cowherds. Mary gave each of them a secret. She appeared and disappeared in a globe of light and moved over the blades of grass without touching them. Celia asked me if Mary was really a virgin.

"She's supposed to be," I told her.

Her eyes widened. She gasped and put her hand over her mouth. "How awful for her," she said.

We drank most of the wine and left the bottle. We went to the picnic, our arms looped together, our faces flushed and laughing, and sat on a grassy bank and watched a band along with the rest of the town: parents and neighbors and little brothers and sisters. There were long tables covered with flapping paper cloths, and food spread out in aluminum tins. Balloons twisted together in the trees. The band sang the Rolling Stone's "Brown Sugar," and little kids stood up and danced, and the grass was trampled from so many people walking back and forth. That afternoon as we sat in the sun Celia told me to keep my eyes open for the boys we'd picked out, and I did, believing I now knew what I wanted from them.

Outside on my curb, I waited for the teenager to come around again, and when I saw him approaching I stood. I smoothed down my blouse. I blocked his path so he would have to stop, which he did, abruptly, without really looking up. His hair covered his eyes. When he did glance at me it was through a veil of black strands. His eyes were large, deeply blue, and arresting.

"Are you lost?" I asked him, a mother offering solace.

He smirked at me. "Why would you ask me that?" he said. His voice was soft and clear.

"You keep passing by here," I told him. I would not be put off, and he seemed amused by my persistence. He stared at me through his hair. His eyes were glazed, unfocused. I knew I could not discern what drug he had been taking. I never knew with my daughter, either.

"Do you want to use the phone?" I asked him.

He smiled. "No," he said. He brought his hand to his face and moved his hair back. His hand was thin and gentle.

"Do you need anything? A glass of water, maybe?" I said. We both stood feeling the wind through our clothes. He hesitated.

"Are you inviting me inside your house?" he asked. "Is that wise?"

I liked him, this doped-up boy. He didn't seem to want anything from me. I owned no small valuables he might covet and pocket. There was nothing he could take that I wouldn't be willing to give. I sorted all of this out before I invited him in. I held the porch screen door for him. His footfalls on the wooden boards were soft, barely perceptible. He paused by the plastic horse Nicholas used to ride. The day he left I had emptied the house of his things, placing them all on the screened-in porch for my daughter to pick up. I saw the horse's springs had begun to rust, and my heart swam and swam. The boy put a hand on its plastic forelock. I opened the door into the living room and he followed me inside.

The room was warm despite the open windows. I inherited all of my grandmother's furniture, but only the smaller pieces fit here. The rest was stored in a climate-controlled storage space two miles away. Sometimes I went there and opened the door and the jumble of furniture—breakfronts and chintz-covered wing chairs and Heppelwhite tables—imparted the smell of her house. Once in a while, the smell inside my own house reminded me of hers. It did at that moment, like wood smoke and lemon-polished maple. I told him to sit down, and he chose the farthest end of the couch. He balanced himself there, his narrow knees jutting out, and looked around.

"Would you like something to eat?" I asked him.

He put his hands on his knees. "No," he said. "I'm not hungry."

He didn't say *thank you anyway.* He didn't seem at all grateful to be there. It struck me, suddenly, that I might not have anything to offer him. I sat in the wing chair opposite the couch. I gave him a small, forced smile, but he would not meet my gaze. I was used to this, with Nicholas. I thought it would be easy to hide how you felt with a child who could not see you. In those first frustrating weeks, when he spilled something over and over, I believed my anger was hidden. And later, after we had put up the swatches of soft fabric for him to touch at the entrance to his room, on his chair at the table, and I watched him find his way around the house, he did not see how I cried over his resolve to please me. But all along he was able to read my silences, to know what I thought by the way I moved through a room, or helped him dress, or set his milk down on the table. He would listen to my voice and know its disingenuous tones and somehow sense below them to the truth.

I sat across from the black-haired boy and looked him over. He was older than I had thought, no longer a teenager, but with the build of one, awkward and lean, unfinished looking. His hands were red-knuckled, resting on the worn knees of his jeans. He kept his face averted, glancing toward the kitchen.

"Where is the kid you live with?" he asked.

The question surprised me. I hadn't expected it from him, and I felt a vague unease.

"He isn't here anymore," I said. I kept my voice level and light. I had answered this question before, posed by the neighbors I passed out walking. They'd noticed I didn't have him with me. They suspected, of course, what had happened. They were hesitant to ask, almost sorry. This boy didn't have that same concern. He stared at me now, with his own surprise. There was a line of tension between his eyes.

"What do you mean?" he asked. He leaned forward a bit, and almost tumbled from the edge of the couch. I saw how unsteady he was, how hard he worked to maintain the appearance of normalcy. My daughter often did the same. We would sit at the table during a meal and the fork would slip from her fingers and clank onto her great-grandmother's Limoges dinner plate. Her eyes slid over me and away, refusing to meet mine. The world she saw, the one her body moved through, was shifting and unclear. I was always touched by her struggle to convince me otherwise.

"He is with his mother now," I said.

I had received a letter from my daughter the other day, detailing Nicholas's adjustments to his school. I knew Renee had told her that corresponding with me was part of her therapy, that it was necessary for Nicholas to keep in touch with me. But we had not arranged any visits yet. I called the number I was given and left messages. I wrote notes that she may or may not have read to him. I reminded him of the day we were at the neighborhood park and there was a loud crash, and the smell of splintered cedar, and I described how a bureau full of clothing had fallen off the back of a passing truck, and balls of socks rolled to the park's chain-link fence, and shirts and underwear flew up and floated down to the sidewalk. Some things, the ones that happen only once, chance things, accidents and mishaps, were the most difficult to describe.

In my living room, the boy leaned back into the cushions of the couch. He tipped his head to view the ceiling and sighed. I stood from my chair then and turned to the kitchen. "I think I'll make some tea," I told him.

"My name is Davy Thompson," the boy said.

"Do you want some tea, Davy Thompson?" I asked. I was in the doorway, looking back at him. I saw his dark hair, the gentle hands, the startling quality of his eyes. Often, we know things and our body reciprocates. This, for example, is a great height and we will not survive if we leap from it. But there are other times our body complicates what we know. Out of old habit it refuses, even, to acknowledge evidence—the tremor of hands, a quickening in the chest, like tiny, beating wings.

"Tea is fine," he said then, his voice still soft with amusement. I went into the kitchen and left him alone while the water boiled. I filled a teapot and let the tea steep. I opened the backdoor to the patio and stood on the stoop and lit a cigarette while I waited. The red amaryllis had come up, the blooms alien and odd on their long, thick stalks. I thought if I left him long enough he would leave, but then he came to the doorway of the kitchen, looking for me.

"You never told me your name," he said.

I exhaled and kept my back to him. "Oh," I said. I still didn't tell it to him. I watched the wind bend the amaryllis, stiff and formal on their stalks. He came up behind me and reached around and took the cigarette from my hand. I watched him bring it to his lips.

"I saw you and the little boy sometimes, in the yard," he said. He smoked and I listened to him talk about the times he'd seen us. I realized I had been too preoccupied then to notice him walking past. I watched him smoke the cigarette down to its filter. Then I went inside to pour the tea. I took the teacups into the living room, and he followed me and sat back down in his spot on the couch. He took the proffered cup with a shaky hand and sipped from it and said nothing more. I watched him look for a place to set the cup down, hesitant to use the coffee table.

"You don't walk every day," I said.

He eyed me and set his teacup, finally, on the wood floor at his feet.

"Only when I need to think," he said.

I felt the breeze from the open window. On it came the jasmine smell.

"And today?" I said.

He leaned back into the couch cushion. He laughed, softly.

"I was trying to decide something." Through the window behind him the neighbor's jacaranda bloomed startling as smoke against the whitish sky.

"And have you, yet?" I asked him. I felt a sense of tumbling, of lost bearings. Davy Thompson shook his head back and forth, slow and weighty, never taking his eyes from me.

I remembered that on the day of the town picnic, Celia and I found the boys we liked and split up. I was still drunk from the wine. I held the boy's hand and we went out into the field. My legs trembled. His palm was soft, and I could not wait for him to touch me, and yet when he did I didn't feel anything. His mouth never fulfilled its predicted wandering. It stayed on mine, or on my neck, wet and sucking, like a snail. There was no undressing. Clothing was pushed hastily aside. The meadow grass scratched and poked. It was all as I had expected, but deadened and flat. Afterward, I could not say I regretted what I'd done. It was as if nothing had happened at all.

I went back to the picnic looking for Celia. I felt in disarray. I felt people's eyes on me, and didn't care. I went around the side of the building, looking for her, though now I wondered if it was her I really wanted to find. It was late afternoon. The band still played, but the sound was muffled, and in the trees of the apple orchard I heard the robins and sparrows assembling before migrating. Along the back of the building was a white painted door, propped open, and inside a narrow hallway and a staircase. I climbed the stairs, quickly, as if they held some kind of escape. In the stairwell I smelled apples, and the polished wood smell of my grandmother's house. At the top a doorway led into a long dormitory with iron bedsteads in two rows, and mattresses covered with ticking. The farthest end of the room was bathed in shadow. The mattresses were thin and stained. The iron frames peeled white paint. Through the dusty windows the sun came in, a watery orange. And then I felt a shift in the air, a pale, silvery alighting, and I saw Celia and a boy on one of the beds, facing away from me and luminous in the shadow like a candle. The boy's hair was tousled, and golden. He was shirtless, his bare back frail and perfect, the skin barely covering the bones. All of my desire rose up like some kind of terrible sadness. I fled from the room, as I had the barn the day I saw Auntie Sister.

Behind Davy Thompson the jacaranda petals rained down, down, onto the street's black pavement. I saw he didn't reach for his teacup. I imagined the liquid grown cold. His eyes were dazed, looking elsewhere. I was reminded of Nicholas in his pose of listening. I would often still myself to hear what he heard. On our walks through the neighborhood we did this together. Our route took us past wind chimes in doorways, the tumbling of laundry in carport clothes dryers, the smell of fabric softener, blooming magnolia, citrus rotting in the grass, cat urine, and trash left out on Wednesdays. We heard the blankness of birdsong, squirrels' claws up telephone poles, the darting of lizards in shrubbery, car engines, hammers of workmen, the footsteps of other neighbors approaching, a stroller's rubber wheels grinding the sandy pavement. And then more—the smell of the juice in the baby's cup, the gum-softened cracker, the wet diaper, the sunscreen, the trace of lily of the valley in the mother's perfume. Layers of life to sense, whole worlds beneath the one we looked at every day.

I told Nicholas everything, but he did not need to hear it. "This," he would say, reaching for what he wanted, frightening me, at first, with his fearlessness. Soon I would grow used to his forays into the yard, to discovering whatever he clutched in his hands. I would trust his desire to know it, to understand its worth and its risk—a piece of a bird's egg, a dead palmetto bug, the shard of china from a pitcher I threw once years before in a rage at my daughter. I have found that despite myself, in the face of resistance and absence, I cannot withdraw my love.

"Sometimes," Davy told me. "I leave my apartment late at night, and I walk until morning. I see people in their houses waking up, their lights coming on, their lives lit up like movie sets."

He told me how he walked down the neighborhood streets at sunrise, and everything—the cracked pavement, the gray and buckling stockade fencing, the line of trash cans along the sidewalk—was burnished. He said the word, *burnished.* He breathed in heavily.

"Just look at this," he said. He reached into his blazer pocket. His hand emerged, cradling something fragile, which he leaned forward to set on the coffee table. It was a parakeet, its plumage brilliant green and yellow. Someone's pet set loose to die in the grass, the thing I had seen him bend to recover earlier.

"This is the problem," he said, his eyes level with mine. "This—carelessness." He turned his palms up on his knees. In his eyes was a despair I recognized.

That afternoon at LaSalette I had walked around the building through the crowd of townspeople with their ribs and corn and plates of macaroni salad. I went back out into the open field and sat down in the tall grass. I didn't move for a long time. I thought of Mary weeping and glorious. Mary of the pyrotechnics, the flash pots, the levitation, the magician's cloak. Mary with her makeup running, unconsummated and sorrowful, her desire a flood, a river overflowing. I imagined her powder-blue garment touching the earth and small green shoots appearing, new grass, mayflowers, slender speedwell, dandelions. I felt the grass move around me and the wide expanse of sky. I felt my body, small and useless and yet lacking nothing. And I knew there was something to believe, that it had to do with all of my longing, my body's hard, bulb-like promise, and if I waited, patiently, it would come to me.

It didn't that day. I went home at dusk through the woods to my house. I lived my life on and on and never knew what I waited for.

Outside my little bungalow the cold day stayed gray. The breeze rattled the screen door. It sent the jacaranda petals upward and out to spread onto my front walk. A car passed. The mailman thumped onto my porch and I heard the hinges of the mailbox. The grayness outside moved into the room. Lately, I had begun to let evening fill the house. I watched the things around me dissolve, the darkness benevolent, a color of forgetfulness. I imagined this, the way it would devour me in the wing chair, balancing a teacup on my lap, my white blouse the last to fade. It would spread to Davy on the couch, swallow him up with his dark hair and clothes. We would be invisible to each other then, though our hearts still beat, our bodies pulsed warmth, separated by what we could not see of the other. I reached up and turned on a lamp, left the wing chair and went to the black-haired boy on the couch. I knelt down beside him in the circle the lamp cast. I saw how beautifully the light included us.

"Give me your hands, Davy Thompson," I said.

They were already there, waiting, smelling of pennies and rising dough, and I took hold of them and placed them on my face. "Now, close your eyes," I told him. Sometimes, you cannot go on with them open.

confessions

She chose the motels. The first time, they met at the one that sells tropicals in back. There was the handwritten sign up front—A Plethora of Plants—and old, fifties-looking neon flashing Sunny South Motel. Just one strip of rooms with doors the color of a nail polish she once liked back when she wore sundresses with little ties on the shoulder, when she had dreamed of having a daughter and smooth muscled arms from lifting and holding her. Peachy-pink, the inside of a whelk. How she had wanted him. How that drove her there, the wanting maneuvering the car beyond her fear of not knowing, really, anything about him. It was the bright glare of noon. There was the chain-link fence in back, the gate with the bell they rang for the proprietor. He emerged, eventually, from an office in the midst of the nursery plants, tanned and stooped and wearing a straw hat. They stood there waiting, a couple, but still he never knew which they wanted, frangipani or a room. There was a certain number of hours available to both of them. There was the need to get it over with already.

At some point in their history, desire had flooded her. She had kept it to herself, her arms and legs aching with it. She slept less. She grew thin. There he was, on a weekly basis, committed, like herself, to someone else with whom vows had been recited in front of witnesses or the eyes of God. Paperwork had been filed. Finances meshed. For her, there was always the difficulty in getting out of it. Years had gone by before she met him. A languishing despair had set in. She was still not sure how he knew. Had he caught her looking? Had he seen on her face some evidence of her longing? Once he discovered her interest, his wish to experience her body began, a mindful reeling-in with messages contrived to win her. Comments on the way her hair fell in her face, the color and texture of her blouse. A whole other world took shape. His idea of her, her idea of him. Things converged.

The first time it was all business. Nothing subtle. This went here, that fit this. It wasn't a mystery, sex. Outside the window they could hear the bell on the gate, the proprietor pitching five-gallon jasmine, papaya, and Japanese plum. They heard the voice of a woman inquiring, a child's whine. They could both imagine the tug of the child on the woman's arm, the drudgery and selflessness. They heard a man's voice, appeasing, silencing the child, a good father in his Saturday clothes, his topsiders flattening the powdery dirt. In the room the air conditioner dripped rusty water onto the carpet. They lay on the blanket they never pulled back. Their legs were tangled. Their bodies slick.

"Now what?" she said.

"Why are you whispering?" he asked.

They had been mostly quiet. There were things she had wanted to say, her mouth pressed to his ear, along his neck, but hadn't. She felt she had not taken advantage of the moment. There were the other usual things she had planned never to reveal about herself, and these overwhelmed her in the finished space, in the silence of not knowing what to say next. The two of them were nearly without introduction. No more than a hundred words had ever passed between them. She had guessed some things, imagined others. He seemed confident about her, a strong supposer of who people were. Whatever else he thought he had invented for his own pleasure.

Missing were the hours of putting the pieces of each other together over dinner or in a car driving to destinations. Absent were the precursors, the gazing, the pinning down of faces to memory, the hand-holding, the quick but potent kiss at the door. They dispensed with that. There was no opportunity, no place absent of potential discovery. And they agreed none of it was necessary. He would never save her from her life. She would never make a mark on his. Their meeting would always be a respite, a dalliance. She lay in the dim room on the blanket. She kept her hands on him as she might a claimed package. She could not predict anything she would take away from this, any moment she would remember later. Already, it had become a blur. Sex in a room. The linens stiff with professional laundering, the dank carpet, the mirrored bureau, the dark television screen like a closed eye.

"What are you thinking about?" he asked.

"Just this," she said, which was not really an answer, and he knew it. But he did not press her further. She thought he assumed she liked it all, which she had, her body almost lifeless on the blanket, her limbs loose, her clothes scattered about the floor, invisible in the shadows and lost to her. "Here I am," she said. "Naked on a bed."

She could see him smile in the dark. If they had a deck of cards they could play gin rummy. The television could be turned on, blaring and brilliant, and something viewed, idly. Up the street was the House of Ribs, an old bungalow nestled among live oaks, where people sat out on the porch to eat, drinking sweet tea out of mason jars. They could drive there and bring back food they would never normally eat, spread it out on the bed in its greasy wrappings, in its Styrofoam packaging. But they had not chosen each other for any of that. She felt her role was limited, and she did not worry about being anything else. She would lie there and wait until she would be of use again. And then he began to fill the silence and she let him. She listened to the timbre of his voice, his cheek pressed to the blanket, the way it became part of the room, competing with the air conditioner, the passing traffic, the squeak of the chain-link gate, the proprietor's movements repositioning the plants on the black tarp.

He gave spare details about himself. He gave his opinion. He gave enough for her to form an impression and a softness for him. Enough, he knew, for her to keep wanting him. He was from a small New England town whose main industry used to be a watch factory. His relatives were all townspeople buried in the old St. Joseph's cemetery. He grew up on a lake, where he boated and skied. He had an older brother who died as a teenager. He had a way about him when he told her, offhandedly, looking elsewhere. She asked few questions, just listened, her body alongside his, her face propped in her hands, her hair spread over his chest.

His brother had cancer. He was sixteen years old, and they had brought him home to die. She saw the house on the lake, its cedar shingles. The dock with its algae-covered pilings, its weathered gray boards. He would have breathed in the smell of the lake through the windows' metal screens, the water in summer cold and filled with particles of debris, sour and brown, the pieces clinging to his skin when he swam. He would have listened to the leaves' dry rustling in the fall, watched them tumble, papery, into the backyard and gather at the lake's rim. Ducks bobbed on the water, even later when the ice formed sheets like glazing.

After his brother's death, he would have read beyond the bland stories in the school textbooks, worried over the ideas, the forces at work, the underpinnings of sitting, still and dazed in a school classroom. The sky would always be an upturned bowl. The freshly painted yellow lines would always mark the tar road. He could go back and still smell the lilacs near the garage, the forsythia tangle up along the house. Those photographs would sit on the same shelf, those motes of dust hover, miraculous, sentient, over the plaid upholstered couch. The longing that struck up in him would last and alter itself to different places, show itself as a different form of impatience. He knew what it meant to tire of something, to discover it and move on.

The afternoon waned. She did not know if she was good at being who he wanted. He was polite and kind and would never admit any disappointment. The worry of losing his interest fell on her as she walked to her car under the flurry of orchid tree petals, through the balm of ginger lily. Who was she now? Her past did not define her. She lived the life she had stumbled onto when she was young and didn't know any better. At some point she had decided there wasn't any better to know. This afternoon she had gotten what she desired, and she pretended she understood what that was, that she had expected nothing else.

The next time it was a place called The Lamplighter. A colonial facade with columns, the rooms stretched out from its sides like two arms, black iron lamppost out front, off of the main road. Years ago, a band that played a local club stayed there, and as a teenager she had gone back to a room with the guitar player. She had put him off, believing then she should first win his love, that he should be made to confess it in the throes of wanting her badly enough, like the other boys. But he had resigned himself to kissing her on the bed, sliding his hand up under her shirt, unzipping his pants and rolling away from her to complete the act that really had nothing to do with her. When she left, he stood with his hands pressed to the plate glass window, half-dressed, watching her with an expression of mild regret. She pretended not to see him. She had gotten lost in the maze of surrounding side streets, amidst the small, squat, cement-block houses still strung with Christmas lights, the overgrown fenced yards, the litter of sun-faded plastic toys, the kiddie pools filled with standing water.

In the heat of summer, the landscape seemed charred and threadbare. The humidity held everything damp and immovable. They met at night, and the windows of the occupied rooms were lit yellow. He had gotten in touch with her after weeks of silence. Nothing was needed beyond this. All of his previously laid groundwork was in place—she still remembered the things he had said to her, the way he looked at her, his mouth on hers, his body without clothes. Along with this she held a small, sad sense of a missed chance she believed meeting him again would eradicate, like an antidote.

He was there first, waiting in the room. He seemed the same, still grinning at her, his eyes with the same ardor. He told her he had not stopped thinking about her.

"What *about* me?" she asked, kicking off her shoes. She did not know if she should have been flattered by his thoughts of her legs, the way her body felt under his, but she was. She was aware that his thinking of her in this way was all she could expect. She doused any other small hopes. She would never tell him the story of the guitar player, fearing he would wonder about her old longing for love, worry that the remnants of it would resurface and complicate what they had. This time, when he held her down on the bed to kiss her, she felt the weight of his hands, the texture of his skin. She felt the soft hairs below his waist when she undid his pants. The room was dark, their bodies hard to pin down. She felt him out with her hands, blindly, seeing with the tips of her fingers, her palms. She saw him in his boyhood bed, its crocheted spread, the lake lapping at the dock outside his window, and the sounds of loons in the morning. She saw him wide awake, listening for his brother dying downstairs in the bed set up in the living room. She saw his baseball cards in a special box with a lid. She saw his row of leather-bound books, the titles in gilt italics. Outside his window, a moon, and the curtains blown out and back, the night air rife with the odor of the afternoon's mown grass.

His hands slid up and down her length. She breathed in their movement, their gentle urging search for her. She stopped them with her own. He looked up at her, puzzled. How to explain that moment before giving in? That quiet "Don't." She could not tell where the resistance came from. But she knew how to back it down, swallow the word, succumb. She knew where to go, which mask to put on. In this way, she avoided the old guitar player story. She circumvented the need for something she would not have, and spared herself.

The room's darkness was broken a bit by the yellow lamplight from outside, its hazy shine through the curtain's join. It left a line across the bed, splitting their bodies in two. He bunched a pillow under his head. His hand never stopped moving, reflexively, over some part of her skin. He looked at her in the dark. She felt his eyes on her, questioning. There was the same air-conditioning noise. A car door slammed outside. Footsteps approached. His hand froze midway up her stomach, and the footsteps passed by, on to another room. She heard him exhale.

"Are you nervous?" she asked, teasing him.

He cleared his throat. "A little," he said, always honest.

She put her hand on his chest and felt the thudding there. She laughed.

"No one could find this place," she said.

The closest main road was two miles away. There was a famous hot dog restaurant where she had told him to turn off. He kidded her about the places she chose. "What about the Holiday Inn?" he'd asked. "Wouldn't a Marriot work?" She told him how she drove around to find the motels, always some reason why she picked the one she did, its proximity to some odd landmark, its kitschy sign, its past popularity replaced with a forlorn look. He told her he liked the hot dog place. It had a big gaudy pink-and-blue sign, rimmed with shiny chrome, studded with lit bulbs. Had she ever eaten there? She told him once or twice, as a child. That was all. Next door to the restaurant was a Dairy Queen where she would have liked to get a sundae with whipped cream. He said, "Do it. Get extra whipped cream." But she did not feel like getting dressed, driving away from him, leaving him behind in the room.

"Come with me," she said.

But he would not budge. He moved his hand up into her hair. He shook his head no, and pulled her face to his and kissed her. "I could taste that on your mouth," he said.

She bit his lip. She slid her body onto his. Sometimes, she thought about him at home with a wife, doing daily things. Sitting at a table with a book, half-listening to her tell a story about people whom they both knew, her hands busy in a sink. Watching her dress in the morning, or at night, flinging off her clothes, and having it mean nothing much. She imagined them together in their bed, covered with the sheet, in sleep, his body turned toward her, or away, his body touching hers, or not. It did not bother her to imagine these things. She did it once in a while to remind herself he was someone already loved.

He told her a story about waterskiing once with his brother. He was eleven. His brother fifteen. Their parents let them take the boat out on the lake and watched from the porch. It was an eighteen-foot Chris Craft, he said. It had been his father's boat, a wooden classic, a 1952 Runabout. He knew how to handle the boat, but on this day, for some reason he still could not explain, the throttle stuck as he turned to pick up his brother bobbing in the water. The engine gunned, he swerved in time to avoid hitting him, but one of the skis was tossed up and struck his brother on the head. There was a lot of blood. He was unconscious at first, still bobbing in his life vest, a darker circle spreading out in the muddy brown lake water.

She listened to the story. She already knew the brother hadn't died then. But still, to hear him, it seemed he believed he had. His voice was awed, the words small, hesitant sounds.

"It turned out alright," she said.

"That time," he told her. He readjusted the pillow under his head with his balled fists. He was resentful, angry. He stopped talking. She got the feeling he would have liked him to die then. That he should not have been made to fear the event twice. She hadn't known what to say to him. She saw he lived with an unremitting expectation of loss, part of himself held in a deep and untouchable reserve. She set herself to his body, as if she was hungry. She distracted him from the past and he returned to her and the bed and the quiet room and attended to his relentless need, his face above her beautifully cruel, until it was time to go.

The Lamplighter was surrounded by what was once a stand of long-leaf pine, invaded now by laurel and turkey oak. There was still one pine left in the middle of the circular drive, its tall trunk impervious to flame, its crown of long needles falling soft and aromatic, onto the hoods of their parked cars. Outside, he would not touch her. He did not say he would see her again. She was prepared to see him or not see him, and she ignored him climbing into his car, the sound of the engine, the sweep of his headlights pulling away. She brushed the pine needles from her hood with her arm, slowly, taking her time, waiting in the dark, though for what she wasn't sure. His headlights circling back? Something else from him? A word, a moment she would not forget, some miracle falling out of the sky, through the ancient pine boughs, onto her body waiting tense with its own promise.

They met again throughout that year. Once or twice at the motel in the orange grove with its gift shop and produce stand on the side, its round, ripe oranges advertised on a peeling wooden sign. The orange blossom smell would get caught in her hair. He would keep his face there, breathing it. A few times at the New Orleans, a two-story motel with ironwork balconies, with rumors of mob hits, surrounded by strip malls and marquees. Next door was the Space Odyssey, a strip club with a replica of a flying saucer on top, where they had seen the girls arriving for their afternoon shift, the sun on the asphalt radiating heat, making their faces wax-like in their makeup. Another time at the beach, at a place with a large plaster Buccaneer and a miniature golf course next door, the metal of the door corroded with salt, the windows stuck shut, and everything mildewed and smelling of the Gulf. They had listened to the tide move out, the long, withdrawing over sand and pebbles and coquinas. Eventually, he said he could not see her anymore, and she assumed he had met someone else, had tired of it all, which she had expected, half-dreaded. She had not risked anything to keep him.

Secretly, she had mapped and unmapped her own life on his body. He could not see in the dark. He had no way of knowing how much of her she left like silver trails and then erased. She was unsure why the burden of the past followed them there, to the room. Why he always told her something he had not thought about in years, how each irreversible error she had made traveled with her into his arms. How she would keep it all in check, saying nothing. Yet she saw, clearly, he was someone in whom she had invested the whole explanation. She asked him for one last meeting, at the first place with the nursery in back. He had agreed. "I'll buy you a keepsake plant," he said. There was nothing sentimental about it. They had uses for each other that prevented that.

They met and it was afternoon again, almost a year later. The orchid tree petals blew down, a violent splash on the concrete. The odor of the plants, yellow poinciana, camellia, and sweet viburnum, followed them into the room. They didn't think of it as the last time. It was just the same as any of the others. He still appreciated her body, more so now, out of nostalgia. They had their own history. They had times before that set precedents, they had moments particular to certain meetings. She knew his loneliness, his longings, the places to move her mouth that pleased him, how to lie, when to hold still, how much to say. He was still the boy in the house on the lake, in the town with narrow roads and clumps of mayflowers and galvanized mailboxes. He still carried some guilt for the loss of his brother, desperate and self-serving. His eyes glowered with it. The muscles in his arms tensed to fight it off. She still eased him into the present, her body making its invisible mark, her own past held at bay. Out of respect, he granted her this silence. To prod her would be a false step into some form of caring, which they both knew to avoid.

They stood apart from each other in the room, and he smiled at her. He never reached for her first. He always waited. She had to show him that her desire was not something she could suppress, that it filled her lungs like a long intake of breath requiring release. She had to say she wanted him, aloud, always meaning it, never like a line she knew she was supposed to speak. She smiled back, revelatory, corroborative. Something he could read and know she meant. She would say what she wanted and not hesitate to slide his shirt up, to touch his skin, to take his face in her hands and just look at him. He let her do all of this. Then, he told her it was his wife, that she had suspected, and at her urging he had confessed. *Don't be angry with me,* his eyes said.

"I want a ginger lily," she told him.

He let his arms fall and was relieved to have something to give her. He went out the door, the sunlight dropping in for a moment, until the door swung shut. She heard the bell on the gate. She heard him speak to the old man, their footsteps among the nursery plants. When he returned he had the lily, its blooms white and heavy and sweet smelling, the leaves shiny green spears. She took him in her arms, laughing. She felt a small, terrified happiness. The meaning of his confession, its feeling, like betrayal, weighed on her while he took off her clothes, while his mouth found hers, and his hands, softly sliding, drew her in.

She would not admit to loving him. It was too late. She had pledged indifference and made herself a prisoner, trapped in her body's longing for something else. At one time, years ago, she'd thought it was a child. She had imagined it solidly in her arms like a warmth, a reprieve. She imagined the child's hair, its skin, its body growing long and beautiful, its eyes on her, waiting for a sign she feared she would not, finally, know how to give. She had gotten pregnant and then panicked, realizing her error, and she had gone on her own and gotten rid of it, and come to this motel, to the old man in the straw hat who had handed her a key. She had been newly married. She had not told anyone. She had wanted to be alone afterward. She had thought, maybe, she would not return home, that all of her mistakes might be so easily erased, and she would start again.

But the doctor had botched it, somehow, and she had bled too much, awakening on the bed in it all, her surprise a kind of dulled one, mixed with a strange grief. Outside, she heard the old man in the nursery, moving around the plants. She heard the chain-link gate open and shut, its rusty latch. It had been late afternoon. The sun slanted in, hot looking, filled with dust, lighting up the sheets and the bright blood, her clothing wet and stiffened, her arms cold and pale and dampened. She had not been afraid. She had lain there and accepted it, her life ebbing away, a steady pulse between her legs, until the wanting to go on living urged her up. She knew that she would pull herself to the door and summon the old man, that he would come into the room and see the mess and call someone else, that the paramedic's penlight would awaken her and drag her back from where she had been headed, a blank space, palely lit, where she did not ever need to know what she wanted or what she was expected to give. And later, she would be delivered into her old life, the life a debt that had not been satisfied, that had increased now, the ledger expanded to include *one child.*

In the room she saw the sun slip low through the Venetian blinds. She felt his hands glide, kept her mouth on his, wet and soft like a wound. She smelled the lily in the room, its scent moving into the folds of her skin, into the places nothing reached. Her body forged on ahead. It opened itself, it gave an edge to the light. She was not without the knowledge, always, that when they left the room the world they'd made dissolved, transformed to molecules, blood, skin, strands of hair, traces on sheets shaken out by maids. The moment no longer existed to hold anything of them together, the lake's lapping water, the stillness of the cedar-shingled house, the boy in his childhood bed believing in a last breath, still waiting, inexorably, for some truth to be revealed. What she admitted to him with her body was dismissed by her silence, made unceremonious and absent of farewell. He held his weight above her on the bed. She felt his deference in the tensile strength of his smooth arms and steady legs. His tenderness sprung from deep-rooted mother-love. He looked down at her, his expression heady. *You do not know me at all,* she wanted to say. *I could be anyone.*

the ropewalk

I never named my daughter. She lives with her father on the coast of another state where it snows, and the snow melts as it lands on the salt marsh, on the brackish still water of North Cove, on the gambrel roof of the house we bought together. When she was born I handed her over, a small bundle weighted with sleep. I remember only a red, wrinkled fist, the smell of milk on my blouse. Now, she may have a new mother whose hands smooth down hair I imagine is my husband's color. She has my grandmother's eyes and smells of the lily of the valley that grows, secretly, behind the hedges at the front of the house. She goes out in the dinghy with her father and he tells her the stories of the sea captain's houses—Pratt, Hayden, Bull, and Starkey—of the square riggers and schooners that came to the Essex port, their cargos of ivory and silk, sandalwood and teak. He tells her about the drawbridge and the road through the great meadow. They will take the dirt path and have picnics on the big rock overlooking the river. Her hair is long, to her waist. She writes her name on the rock with a small stone shining with mica. I am filled with longing for this other life, but who knows what I would have longed for if I'd lived it?

Where I work the patrons come in for draft beer and wait for someone to single them out for a game of darts or pool. It might be a weekday or a weekend afternoon, the heat and the sun slipping in through the door with them, the humidity curling the posters tacked to the walls—Thursdays, Ladies 2 for 1, Dollar Draft Friday Nights. It might be the dinner hour, when only a block away people are waiting for a table in the new French Vietnamese restaurant, or sitting down in dining rooms with wives or husbands and children and cloth napkins in their laps. Here in the bar they light up a cigarette and wedge it into the notch in the plastic ashtray and let it burn down, forgetting. They switch to bourbon when it grows dark. They tell me about the women they love, the men they despise, casually, as if it is the most normal thing in the world to love anyone that obsessively, to plot the ruin of someone who has hurt them. They twist the truth to invoke sympathy, or to hide from me their dire need. They are desperate people and they do not know it.

The owner of the Tap Tavern approached me eight years ago and offered me the job. He sat down next to me on a bench in the neighborhood park, newly landscaped with palms and bird of paradise and caladium, its life-sized concrete lions spitting water, and children running through it barefoot, their nannies holding tiny socks and shoes. I felt out of place in my clothes from the evening before. He was a stranger, and I ignored him. It was a December afternoon with a breeze. There is a sculpture in the park made entirely of keys, thousands of them strung on thin, dangling wires that I could hear from my apartment's balcony, and we heard it then, sitting there on the bench. He cocked his head, listening. "Imagine every one of those keys deprived of their tumblers," he said. I looked at him, surprised. I may have smiled, thinking about what he said. He took my hand then, and introduced himself. He had damp palms and wore jeans with bleach stains. A full white beard covered his chin. He held my hand in his endearingly, and squinted at me in the warm winter sun. I remember his hand shook with tremors, and I thought he was a gentle old man who had mistaken me for someone else, or a lonely person seeking solace in conversation. He is none of these things.

His name is Dr. Chambley. At one time he practiced veterinary medicine. He still retains the manner of treating people calmly, as if they, like his animal patients, held the potential of sudden revolt with nails and teeth. Now, he is an alcoholic who imagines himself a poet, who bought the Tap Tavern two days before he saw me on the park bench. He had noticed my silk Prada pumps, the way my slit skirt showed my thighs. His plea for me to tend bar was initially a pickup line, an elaborate one that had me standing that evening in my heels and skirt, pouring draft beer, while he posed as my first customer. He sipped from his frosted glass and told me I looked like the woman in *A Bar at the Folies-Bergere.* The wet glass left water droplets on his beard. He had changed to one of the Brooks Brothers shirts that hang in the small back room, still wrapped in the dry cleaner's blue plastic. I had my own drink beside the well, and I thought the game was slick of him, and I planned to play it all the way through, just to see where it would take me.

I am still here. The Tap Tavern is on a narrow brick-lined street in the heart of a neighborhood built in the 1920s by wealthy citizens. The large two-and three-story bungalows had once known a long period of decline. Paint chipped off wood siding, jaunty striped awnings decayed, porches with elaborate balustrades sagged, and the heart pine floorboards, rare and expensive, succumbed to termites. During this time houses were split into apartments, and less affluent people moved in, and a few eyesores popped up, buildings that now, since the neighborhood has been so impeccably restored, everyone pretends aren't there—a frame shop and an accountant's office hidden by kudzu, overgrown philodendron, and wild, climbing jasmine. They remain signless, known only to the people who have frequented them for years or by word of mouth. The Tap Tavern is one of these, a small, windowless, concrete block building, with an old wooden screen door and an appropriate sense of the forlorn about it.

Inside the door there is no opportunity to assemble yourself to make a good impression, to peruse the crowd without being noticed. There is just the one room, twenty-five feet by fifty—pool tables to the right, bar to the left. Directly in front of you against the wall is a refrigerator, an ancient white Frigidaire that Dr. Chambley inherited from his deceased mother, and between the door and the back wall are some round tables with metal chairs. The floor is pine boards, darkened and swollen with age and spilled liquor. Ceiling fans spin the cigarette smoke overhead. Two air conditioners cool the place off, even in the winter months when the metal door is left open, and the screen door lets in the smell of the neighbor's star magnolia.

I like the odd, homey sense of the place, as if you have just walked into someone's kitchen. I like the people who come every night and the newcomers who pop through the door expecting something else, the looks on their faces, startled, then amused. We get couples in evening clothes, tired of the party at an associate's house. There are young people, tattooed and pierced, and pale, shaking ones who appear at all hours collecting their drugs. And on weekends, the men and women who work in offices as legal assistants, as real estate agents, as secretaries and marketing experts, searching each other out, seated on the stools at the bar. Some of them, like me, live in the apartments made from the old houses. Some live in the newer lofts and townhomes built in the empty lots left by houses that were torn down. They slide their fingers up bare thighs, play with shirt collars, flatten their hands against chests, order pitchers of drinks. They keep me, conditionally, on the fringes of their lives, and I rarely see any of them outside the bar.

Darla isn't an exception. She has been coming here for two years. Her blond hair flips out at her shoulders, 1960s-style. Freckles sprinkle her narrow, upturned nose. She carries herself with a dancer's torso, and I am almost certain she came from a family that taught her to smile at cashiers and cab drivers, and say, "Yes, Ma'am," to anyone older, regardless of class. She wears expensive jeans and flimsy halter tops and looks like she has a regular job, which I know she does not. She lives off the child support provided by her ex, the clothes leftovers from her life before. She has two children, little girls whose fine, white-blond hair she must have had as a child. I have seen the photos she pulls out late at night, when they are supposedly with their father, and she is particularly unhappy with her life.

Sometimes during closing, I am the only one in the bar to show them to, and I try not to reveal to her the wrenching feeling I get looking, or how the photographs of her daughters chart for me the passing of unredeemable time. Other nights, a crowd will gather, kindly and respectful. "This one's Ada," she'll say, pointing her manicured finger, "And this is Lenore." At two a.m., no one can see the images too clearly. But the women will make their cooing noises, sigh, and remark on the girls' beauty, and one of the men will say Darla looks too young to have two children, and another will mention how much they resemble her, to which she will give a watery-eyed smile. "Don't they?" she'll say. She'll fasten her look on the man, and he will know he has scored a point with her, that maybe, since the kids aren't there, she will take him home with her. I am a little saddened that most kindnesses in a bar are calculated, that everything that happens here blooms from the alcohol. There aren't any sudden and unplanned instances of love.

Dr. Chambley is friendly to Darla but he keeps his distance, which surprises me sometimes, because I know his type. I often point out women he might love, and he tries to pick them up. We do not pretend to only want each other, but I choose the women halfheartedly, and when he is successful I feel a vague unease. I find someone from the bar for myself, though I still do not know if he recognizes this as retaliation. One Friday night, after Darla had left and we were ready to close up, I asked him why he didn't go for her.

"Why should I?" he asked me back. He was zipping up the money pouch, a little unsteady on his feet. "She's trouble." He looked me right in the eye, the way he does before he plans to kiss me or take a splinter of glass from my finger.

I stepped back. "She's just like everyone else," I said, though as I said it I realized it wasn't true. The room was smoky, the door was open, and I wanted to get near the air. He took my arm then and turned me around. He gave me the look, wary and serious, of someone considering my best interests. He had lined the empty bottles up on the top of the bar, and turned off the lights and left one of the air conditioners running. Dr. Chambley is annoyingly meticulous at times. He has to follow the same patterns every night, counting the drawer two, sometimes three times, checking the door twice before he walks away. I am never sure if I should trust his advice, knowing these weaknesses. He still has a wife and three grown children and a membership to the country club. He lives four blocks away in one of the renovated bungalows. He was undeserving of his wife's love, he once said. We were in bed in my apartment at the time, on one of the first occasions we'd slept together. He told me my set of rooms was once part of a stucco villa that belonged to the man who brought the Pepsi franchise to the city. The room was dark, and the streetlight came in through the old casement window glass, and the air conditioner hummed from the other room.

"Whose love do you deserve?" I asked him. I slid my body over his, pressed my forehead to his chest.

He laughed. "No one's."

"Why is that, do you think?"

He sighed. "Don't try to figure yourself out with my story. Go to sleep now." But his presumption angered me. I grabbed my clothes and slammed the apartment door and dressed on the stair landing, in the light of a weak, yellow bulb and the neighbor's cooking smells. I went down the stairs and out into the courtyard and knew that up in the room he was still in my bed, expecting me to come back, that at that moment I might choose to return to the room and tell him my story, listen to myself telling it and understand, finally, what I ever meant by my leaving, feel his mouth on mine afterwards like forgiveness. But I did not, and then he came down the stairs and got into his car and left, and I missed, instantly, the softness of the bed, the weight of him balancing the mattress. I missed the smell of his fingers, like limes, the way they smoothed the hair from my forehead. You can miss anything, I saw. It didn't mean it made you happy.

That night after I mentioned Darla, Dr. Chambley and I stood together in the parking lot. He did not offer me a ride home, which meant that he did not want to sleep with me. It was summer, and the air was heavy. Thunder rumbled, distant and almost comforting. My apartment was only a block away, close enough for me to walk. I did not usually drive to work. Dr. Chambley always drove the four blocks back and forth to his house in an old Stingray convertible he bought after he sold his practice. On the nights I had someone waiting for me, Dr. Chambley would walk purposefully to his car, preoccupied with his keys, and he did that now, though there was no one waiting. I wished there was someone to lure into my life, to take home and wonder what he thought of me, watch his face during sex with the detachment you get watching an accident happen to someone else. The crumbled shells of the parking lot shone white and bleached in the streetlight. I dreaded the walk home, abandoned to the night's looming rain, the interminable sound of the sculpture's keys marking the empty place Dr. Chambley made when he chose not to be with me.

A few nights later, Darla came in early, at five o'clock. I felt the afternoon heat come through the door with her, smelled it clinging to her bare arms and shoulders, heady as her Guerlain. She had already been drinking. I smelled that on her, too. She put her arms around me and hugged me hello. She wore her hair plaited in two small braids. I imagined the little girls at home with their plates of SpaghettiOs and bread and butter, sitting in front of the television alone. She would have given them their bath and patted them each with powder. The evening news was on the TV over the bar. Darla lit up one of her long, thin cigarettes. She offered me one, and I took it, and as she leaned in with her lighter I saw her eyes well up, and as she sat back I saw she had begun to cry.

"Beau's trying to take the girls away," she said. She wiped under each eye with a finger to stop her mascara from running.

Beau was Darla's husband. We had never talked about him before. I just remembered the name from times she had used it in passing. "Beau took the girls to Sanibel," she'd said. "Beau's mother is getting the girls' ears pierced today," she told us all once with a wounded pout. "Don't you think that's my department?"

Tonight, I made Darla her old fashioned and brought it over to where her cigarette burned in the ashtray, and she sat with her face in her hands. I touched one of the braids with my fingers. I knew I wouldn't have to say anything, that I could just listen to her while she had her drink, and the place would fill, and someone else would appear to tell the story to, and I would overhear it told two or three, maybe four times before she left, each telling revealing the variety of ways in which she is taken advantage. The regular patrons would all offer their advice, and some of it would be good, and some wouldn't, but none of it would matter. Darla, I assumed, would end up doing nothing, and her life would simply happen to her. Sometimes, I know, this comes as a relief, this resignation, this kind of surrender.

Years ago, I took the walking tour of the town where my husband and I bought our house. He had grown up there, and I knew no one, and he was often away on business. I was visibly pregnant, and the guide, a retired man, kept glancing back at me with a nervous smile. Our small group made its way down Pratt Street in the new spring light, beside the patches of bright grass, beneath the wheeling of gulls, and he told us the story of the old ropewalk. It was eight hundred feet long, he said, raising his arms to show the span, a low wooden shed with small windows. Inside, the workers made rope by hand, twisting the hemp into heavy hawsers, into bell ropes and string used for kites, the room alive with ropes spun from the great wheel. They made the rope for ships in fathom lengths, drawing it through the doorway and out into the street. The guide recited Longfellow, "Human spiders spin and spin, Backward down their threads so thin," and I remember his voice, how the sun was warm on my head and shoulders, the way the wind sounded in the elm leaves. We paused at my husband's family's house, and the guide pointed out its handsome federal style, its roof's shallow pitch, its double chimneys, its original owner who ran the block and spar business. I stood outside of the house on the sidewalk with the others, marveling. In the end, I would not choose that life, its wealth and history like a closed wheel, but standing there at the time I did not know it yet. I felt only a small swell of uncertainty, the baby's kick, my heart's quickening. In the Tap Tavern, my hair full of smoke, and my hands smelling of spilled bourbon, I knew that the ropes were like lives stretched out infinitely into the sunlight, that it didn't matter which life you picked. The one you didn't was yours anyway, drawn out alongside the one you lived like a possibility.

"He says I'm *incompetent,"* Darla whispered. She gave me a wide-eyed look, and bit into a piece of ice. "He thinks I'm neglecting them."

We both knew she was neglecting them, but we maintained the pretense that she was not, that her love for them cancelled out all irresponsible actions on her part. I put on my shocked expression. I lit another cigarette. And the place filled up, and I became too busy to placate her. Dr. Chambley came in later, and she was still at the bar, and he sensed her story in the air, like the fine, silver tension before a fight. He cornered me at the back of the bar and asked me what was happening. His eyes glittered in the light from the beer sign. He wanted the satisfaction of seeing a prediction fulfilled, and I did not want to hand it over to him. But I knew he would find out from someone, and so I told him.

He watched my face with his penetrating look. Most of the time, I loved this about him. "And what will she do?" he asked me.

I shrugged. "She didn't say."

"Because," he said, "she doesn't have a leg to stand on."

We had never disagreed about anyone in the bar before. It was never an issue to care about them too much. When her husband sent in someone the following night to inquire about her visits to the bar, I avoided him. I did not want to tell the truth, but Dr. Chambley was there, listening, and there were other regulars the man talked to, and it wouldn't have helped for me to lie. The man fit in, and had seemed like a new patron at first. He wore a seersucker sport coat. His hair was thinning, and he kept flattening it with his hand. His nose was large and he was perspiring. I thought he was a drunk, a salesman, a traveler. We get those, occasionally, as if there is some kind of beacon on the place. He gave me a sad, conciliatory smile, and leaned on the bar's surface, his coat sleeve sopping up the condensation from his beer.

"She pretty wasted when she leaves?" he asked.

His upper lip shone. His eyes moved, for a moment, toward the V of my blouse. I glared at him, and did not speak. He waited until my silence forced him to turn away. Later, Dr. Chambley pulled him aside and they talked for a long while sitting at the corner of the bar. I shoved the bottles into the well with unnecessary force. Two glasses slipped from my hands and shattered in the metal sink. I went up to a man at the bar, a regular customer with long hair pulled back, and round framed glasses. He'd been trying to take me home for weeks, and I'd always resisted. Tonight, I leaned over and kissed him on the mouth and tasted the drink I'd made him. At closing, Dr. Chambley confronted me, holding my hand in his two palms.

We stood in the dark bar and the man waited for me outside in a Riviera, and I wanted to taste the drink on his mouth again, feel the car's vinyl seats, his hands search beneath the fabric of my blouse, under the hem of my skirt. I could take him home and watch to see if he looked at my books on the shelf, if he commented on the absence of photographs, on the bare and simple way in which I lived. Or, we could do what we needed to in the car, right there in the parking lot. Afterward, I would have him drop me off, and I could pass through the courtyard and listen to the old fountain, see the basin of rusted pennies in the moonlight, smell the gardenias, listen to the keys of the sculpture, their sound a mournful reminder of the life that I was missing. Sometimes, I wallowed in it like the sadness of a mistake.

Dr. Chambley gave me his inquisitive look. "What's this Darla business got to do with you?" he asked.

"Nothing at all," I said. Dr. Chambley watched me. He didn't make a move to leave. I saw him lick his lips and glance away, befuddled for once. I had to tell him I had someone waiting in the parking lot. He still looked, hoping for some revelation.

"Do you know what I really want?" he asked. He made a careful business of folding up his shirtsleeves. He breathed in and out, emphatically. "Some honesty, for once." His eyes were worn and dismayed. We went out the door and he went back and checked the handle, twice, and got into his Stingray. He didn't give me a backward glance. I was left with the taillights of the Riviera, its chugging engine, its foul exhaust spilling out, my own regret at what I might always fail to give him.

Two weeks later Darla came in at nine o'clock, towing her girls. They wore matching nightgowns, long ones that came to their shins, made from batiste. They followed their mother, the oldest shy, yet alert, the youngest one half-asleep, her eyes lit with fear. Darla came up to me at the bar and gripped my forearm.

"Please," she said. Her lined eyes were wide, the mascara smeared a little under each. The bourbon smell came through her skin's pores. The little girls climbed up on two empty stools. I saw their small faces framed by their whitish hair. I noticed their hands on the bar, the little fingernails, painted pink. I smelled their apple shampoo. The oldest, Ada, was seven. Lenore was five. They both looked at me, curious, expectant, their eyes replicas of their mother's, blue-green, like something sea-washed and soft. Dr. Chambley had not come in. He sometimes didn't until eleven or twelve, and Darla knew this.

"Let them stay," she said. "Their father is coming to take them away, and I can't leave them at home." She said this last part leaning in, as if to prevent the girls from hearing, but she did not lower her voice, and I saw they heard and already knew what was happening. They lived in a small rented house I had seen the few times Dr. Chambley and I dropped Darla off after closing. I had thought about the girls in there alone, what they would wake to in the morning, with Darla stumbling in, sometimes passing out right there in the living room on the couch, or the rug. I thought, too, about how I had served her the drinks and I felt a small tug of complicity. But now, with the girls in front of me, their breath and skin, their sheer nightgowns, their little feet shod in flip-flops tucked on the top rung of each barstool, I felt my chest constrict.

The oldest, Ada, asked me for a Coke. I was surprised that she asked, but then I understood she was asserting herself with me, showing me she was grown up, that she was the one who woke her mother, and got her out of her soiled clothes, and made meals, and handled everything at home, and so I gave it to her, without a word. The youngest was silent, still frightened and somewhat pale.

"Would you like anything?" I asked her. The bar was almost full, noisy with the games of pool and darts. The air conditioners were on, but it was still smoky, and I saw her eyes begin to water.

"She'll have a Sprite," Ada said. Lenore nodded, and Ada placed her hand over her sister's on the bar.

Darla, distracted, glanced around the room, looking for a regular to confide in, to seek advice, to find some kind of aid. She lit a cigarette. She met my gaze and her eyes asked me for a drink, and apologized at the same time. Darla was beautiful with a hopeless and shining desperation. She sighed. She looked at my shoes, the Prada pumps that won Dr. Chambley. "I like those," she said, wistfully. She blew smoke out of her nose. Her lips were thin and dry. She looked at her two girls with a love so resigned I had to look away.

My husband bought the Prada pumps at Neiman's. They were a gift at the end of my pregnancy. The salesclerk had raised her eyebrows at the stiletto heels. The department store had been over-bright and sterile, filled with the smell of new carpeting and spray samples of perfume from the nearby fragrance counter. "For after," my husband said, grinning, his tie loosened, his throat pale and vulnerable under his collar. The idea of the places I would have to wear them, how I would wear them to please him, overwhelmed me. I realized I had not thought beyond the pregnancy, that I could not bear to live the life he had planned for me. I did not want him anymore. It was a simple thing to recognize, this lost love, as if it had slipped underneath some hidden layer of my life and I could not find it. And still his love persisted. I was pinioned by it, bound and helpless under the department store's fluorescent lighting.

In the Tap Tavern, Darla sipped from her drink. She picked it up and set it back down with a shaky, slender hand. Ada watched her, and then glared at me for a long time, and I saw she blamed me. She was a little girl, but her eyes were wise and sad, and I knew then that maybe a life with their father would be better for them, but it would never replace the one they would live with Darla, her attention, her lovely hands in their hair, her fearful eyes on them, needy for their honest professions of love.

Darla sat at the bar and cried. The girls were used to her crying, and they seemed almost disinterested, preoccupied with the stirrers in their glasses.

I let them stay, a mistake I can admit to now. At the time, it seemed the only thing to do. None of the other patrons minded. We put on a movie on the TV over the bar, one that was only partly appropriate, and they propped their heads in their hands and watched. The patrons coughed loudly or placed tobacco-stained fingers over the girls' eyes when an actor swore or during a love scene. Someone brought them bags of potato chips. Someone else gave them lollipops that stained their lips red. Lenore dribbled her Sprite down the front of her nightgown. Darla sipped her one drink, making an effort not to overdo it. And the patrons gave her advice. Some told her to give them up, that it was the only way she'd ever see them again. Darla's eyes grew puzzled. I saw that this had not ever occurred to her, that giving them up was something she could not understand and I admired her foolish resolve.

Lenore fell asleep at the bar, her head on her folded arms. I waited for Dr. Chambley, for her husband to come in and find them. I had expected he would, that they would search for them here first, but Darla confided in me that she had left a note claiming she had taken the girls to Orlando, to her mother's.

"Just to buy time," she said.

"Where will you really go?" I asked.

Darla put her mouth to my ear. "Louisiana," she said. "To my best friend's house in Shreveport."

I was surprised that she had a plan, that she was so calculating. I thought then that she might succeed, that she would get away with keeping them despite the husband's sober authority, his judge's order. Darla looked at me and smiled, tentatively. She put her two hands out and held my face in them, a mother who knew how to administer love.

"I'm going to keep them," she said. "No matter what."

When you are alone, you become used to not being touched. You become suspicious, and learn not to relent. Maybe, you let one person take you in, like Dr. Chambley, a man of extreme patience, with practiced hands. But even then, it is only partway, only a piece of yourself you give up, your body during sex, and that is it. Darla let her hands fall. I glanced away and busied myself with stacking the glasses, with the patron at the far corner, sliding off his barstool. I would not look at Ada, whose eyes followed my movements with a silent expectation. Somewhere, in a town I fled, a child I might have known slept. She would have a bed with cotton sheets and a blanket, even now in summer. I know the smell that comes through the window screen, chilled and sharp, the flowers beginning to fail in their blooming. I know the room where she sleeps, with its dormer window and its eastern exposure. I see the sun on her face. I see, too, her chest moving with her breathing. Her hands are still small and childish-looking, grasping the edge of the sheet. She is only eight and unburdened with worry. Her dreams tell her nothing about me. I am not even an absence to be missed. I am unremembered.

Near the end of the night, Dr. Chambley came in. He stood in the doorway and his eyes lit on me, filled with a curious disappointment. He told Darla, "in no uncertain terms," that she must go with the girls.

They were both asleep by then, and one of the patrons carried Ada slung over his shoulder, her little batiste gown sliding up her skinny legs. Darla carried Lenore, her face buried in Lenore's shoulder so I could not see it. I left the bar and the patrons and their demands, and walked them out to Darla's car, a Mercedes she was awarded in her divorce, battered now, covered with months of dust. I cannot say what compelled me to do this. I watched them all pile in, the two girls in the back, both of them awakened, but groggy, struggling to find comfortable positions amidst the luggage stacked behind the seat. The air was warm and carried the star magnolia and the smell of the cigarette smoke clung to our clothes. I leaned into the driver's side. Darla's mouth was set, a thin line, and she tried to smile to say goodbye.

"Wait," I told her. And I turned and walked past the patrons gathering in the lot with their drink glasses, their bottles of beer, past Dr. Chambley who had now come out to witness their infraction. He raised his hand to take my arm, but I brushed past. Behind the bar I took the bills from the register drawer. All of them, a nice stack of twenties, tens, a few fifties. And I brought the money out to Darla and handed it to her. No one made a move to stop me, not the patrons, whose mouths opened and then closed, giving me their assent. Though I knew the money meant nothing to Dr. Chambley, I expected he would object to the principle of giving it away, of aiding their escape, and I dared him to stop me, like one of the dogs in his old office, its teeth bared. Darla took the money from my hand, her own hand soft and lingering on my arm. The car idled, and I felt the air-conditioned space inside. The girls called goodbye, their small voices rising out of the darkness of the backseat, and Darla put the car in drive.

I sway and totter on my heels, watching the taillights disappear, knowing I cannot call them back. The car hurtles away. It will stop at service stations with unkempt and despairing attendants. The girls will eat small packaged doughnuts coated with confectioner's sugar. I can only hope Darla will not panic and pull over for a drink. I feel a blinding terror for them, encased in the metal of the car, their delicate limbs, the veins and skin covering them, their soft mouths, their wildly beating hearts. There is no surety, no safety, just Dr. Chambley's eyes on me, his hand reaching out to steady me where I stand on the crumbled shells, ready to be loved.

pins and needles

It began in snow. Annie met him outside of Wegman's. He pulled off his knit hat and spun around when he saw her. His friends kept walking toward their car, making groaning sounds, like they were used to this. The snow made lacy patterns on his peacoat's shoulders. She didn't like the way he wet his lips before he talked, as if he worked hard over what to say to her. What he had to say to her didn't matter. He was a boy from the college, and she was a married woman with a newborn. Her husband was home waiting for a can of tomato soup and some saltines, and her baby was sleeping. The furnace thundered on in the damp basement. Dust skirted the kitchen's linoleum threshold. Outside the windows the snow fell cleanly on ragged cornfields. All of this went on while the college boy spun in his tracks.

He held his hat to his heart. He had a southern accent she thought, at first, was fake.

"Darlin'," he said. He wet his lips.

She stared at him, surprised. Later, she would not be asked what made her do it, but if she had she would have said that his calling her *darlin'* wasn't it. As she stood in the falling snow, watching the college boy press his hat to his heart, she had a feeling. She waited, watching him. The bag boys with coats thrown over their smocks slid in their boots around the parking lot, retrieving the carts. The blown snow melted on her cheek.

"It's cold out here," she said, sounding like the girl she used to be in high school—aloof, impatient.

"I'm wondering . . ." he said, slowly, dropping his hat to his side. His voice was mannered and low. She thought of southern things she'd seen in movies—plantations, and pecans weighing down branches, and azaleas flourishing along white-painted porches. Women brushed past them, intent with their shopping lists. Their coats smelled of apples, or wood smoke, or roasting meat. It was a Sunday. That morning, she'd listened to the Presbyterian church's bells and thought the snow falling made them sound different. She'd sat on the couch in their rented house and waited for the baby to wake up. Her husband worked early each morning distributing the *Cortland Standard,* then day shifts at the nearby Clark's Market, slicing deli meat. Her mother told her to sleep when the baby slept, but Annie always awoke—this time with the snow falling into the streetlight's beam, to the passing of the long trucks carrying tree trunks on Route 13, to the windows shaking in their frames. She thought she'd heard noises on the back porch—someone stomping snow off their shoes, trying the storm door, quietly depressing the latch. She sat with her hands clenched in the sleeves of her sweatshirt, scouting the room for ready weapons.

"I'm wondering, too," she said to the boy. "I'm wondering who you think you are to stop me, and talk to me like this."

He wet his lips in earnest, the words he wanted to say caught somewhere below their surface. She felt sorry then, and she shifted her feet and sighed. She turned and would have taken the step that triggered the automatic door into the store, but he reached out and took her sleeve, and she stopped and looked back.

"Don't go," he said. He was sincere, and then embarrassed. She saw these things mark his face in succession.

"Why?" she asked him.

He hesitated. She saw his eyebrows come together. "You'll think I'm crazy, but you look exactly like my dead girlfriend."

She paused. She pushed her hands deeper into her pockets, and looked out at the snow covering up car hoods and windshields, lying piled and perfect on the Meadow Street guardrails. Back at her house it blanketed the rusted car that refused to start, the shed with its fallen roof, the row of trashcans, the decaying firewood, the bed frame and mattress they slept on before her mother bought them a new one. The snow blew under the ill-fitting storm windows and into the house's windowsills where it melted and pooled. She had chosen to drive here, fifteen miles from Clark's. She had not meant to, but she had gotten into the car and found herself on Main Street, passing Moss's funeral home and the Agway, then over the bridge, unable to suppress the impulse to keep driving. All along Route 13 the snow drifted across the pavement like sand. Now, it clung to cars' tires, and the tires made a dull crunching sound as they passed.

"When'd she die?" she asked, doubting him, but pretending not to.

"August," he said. His voice, solemn sounding, had a honeyed ring. She imagined him clutching a girl's fragile hand on the white-painted porch, the night balmy and scented with wisteria.

"What happened to her?"

He shook his head, and looked down at his boots.

"Oh. I see. You can't talk about it," she said.

He must have sensed then that she didn't believe him. He looked up at her, his eyes beseeching and sorrowful. The way he looked at her stung her. As if it might even be true, that she resembled a dead girl he had once loved. They stood this way, letting the snow melt on their sleeves. The cars' tires crunched past. The people chose their steps carefully across the parking lot. The smell of snow was strong in the air.

"Your friends will be waiting for you," she said.

"So?" he said.

And then the car pulled up, and the passenger window slid down, and his friend called out to him through a cloud of exhaust, "You coming?" and the boy waved him away and turned back to her. She watched the car drive off, its taillights red at the stop sign, the tires sliding a bit when it accelerated out of the lot.

"I have to go," she told him.

"Why?"

His face looked pained. Even his single-syllable words sounded like music. He kept his eyes on her face, looking for something.

"What exactly do you want?" she asked him. She tugged her arm free from his hand.

"I'm not sure," he said.

"Would you like to know my name?" she said.

"It's not Katie Beauchamp," he said softly, sadly.

And she closed her eyes for a moment, feeling something indefinable. "What if it was?" she said. "Is that what you want?"

His face changed, and she imagined his heart thudding beneath his wool coat.

"Where do you live?" she asked him.

He explained he was house-sitting for a professor. He asked if she would give him a ride there. She tipped her face up and felt the snow on her mouth.

"No," she said. "I don't think I will."

They stood there a moment longer. She didn't care that his friends had abandoned him. She stepped away and the door sprang open. The smell of baked bread came out.

"Katie would never have left me like this," he said.

She stopped and turned back to him. His face had reassembled itself. He held his arms lifted, and his coat's shoulders bunched up. She knew that when she came out he would still be there, and when she drove away he would watch her. That when she heated up the soup at the stove in her drafty kitchen, slipped the bottle's nipple into her daughter's tiny mouth, she would see his eyes, his brownish hair. When her husband slid across the sheets to her out of reluctant need she would remember his wet lips, the timbre of his voice. It was already done, she saw.

She drove him home. He sat beside her in her husband's car, fiddling with the bottle opener he'd found in the console, the crushed pack of cigarettes.

"So you're a smoker and a drinker," he said, laughing, holding the things in his two hands.

"Those aren't mine," she said.

He pressed the car lighter in and when it popped out he held it to the corner of the cigarette pack and watched the cellophane smoke.

"Stop that," she said.

His coat smelled of wet wool. He gave her directions, but he didn't say anything else. The house was a red shingled two-story in Lansing. It was an older, renovated home, with new casement windows and a black-painted door. The driveway had been plowed, but the falling snow filled it in.

"I appreciate the ride," he said.

He got out of the car and went up the cleared path to the front door. The times she was dropped off her ride always waited to be sure she got in safely, so she did this now, the car's exhaust chugging out. She saw him hesitate at the door, and then turn, and come back down the walk. He opened the passenger door and leaned in.

"You want some hot cocoa?" he asked her.

She looked at his hopeful face, and then behind him to the house. No one in the world knew where she was. "Is that what Katie liked?"

"It sort of goes with the weather," he said. "She'd never experienced snow before."

She turned off the car and slid the keys into her pocket. She followed him up the walk to the door.

"Have you ever experienced snow before?" she asked him.

"No," he said, turning to her. They stood face to face. The front of their coats touched. "This is my first."

She felt his breathing on her cheek. Then, he turned back to the door and fitted in the key. Inside it was warm and immaculate. The door opened onto the staircase. To the right was the living room, the couches upholstered in cream-colored fabric. Potted plants lined the top of a bookshelf. A baby grand piano stood in a corner, and shelves of old-looking books, the titles on their spines in faded gilt, took up one wall. An Oriental carpet covered the wood floor. They slipped off their shoes at the door, and she followed him into the kitchen. A set of sliding glass doors looked out onto a wooden deck. The backyard was a wide, white expanse that connected to the various neighbors' yards. To the right on a trailer sat a huge boat with a brilliant green bottom, the color of photos she'd seen of the sea in the Caribbean. The snow fell gently onto its tarp.

He stood and looked out at the yard, the boat. He shook his head. Then he turned to her.

"It's a Bertram," he said.

She nodded. On Cayuga Lake, fishing with her father when she was small, she'd seen all kinds of boats, but this one seemed built for something else—a seacraft, a yacht intended for long passages. Its name, painted on the back, was *Pins and Needles.*

"It's the professor's ex-husband's," he said. "Well, hers now."

The boat stood under a stand of pine, their branches soft as brooms laden with snow. Annie said "Oh." She didn't know what else she was supposed to say.

"Hard to believe that last summer we played croquet on that lawn." He turned back to the kitchen and perused the cabinets. "I'll admit I have no idea how to make cocoa." He shrugged off his coat, and held out his hand for hers. She handed him her coat, and he hung them both on pegs on the opposite wall.

"We don't really need it," she said.

He slid onto a stool and folded his arms on the countertop. He wore a heavy, wool sweater that looked hand knitted. She had on the T-shirt she'd slept in and a pair of old jeans. She stood by the porch door and felt the cold radiate off the glass.

"So," he said.

She looked at him. "Yes?"

He laughed. She smiled back. "Come here," he said.

This was a nice boy, from a good family, she determined. He had a wishful hope that she had come for sex, and she admitted to herself that maybe she had, but she knew she would not give in so easily, even if it was what they both wanted. She turned back to the view of the backyard.

"So, you were here in the summer?" she asked.

She heard him slip off the stool, felt him move up behind her.

"Yeah," he said. "Melissa, the professor, was in England. She's in Islamorada right now."

He put his hands on her shoulders. He was cautious with his hands' placement. She let them stay there, warming her up.

"She forgot her boat," she said.

The boy laughed. "She got that in the divorce. She hates boating. It was her husband's way of evening the score."

She felt his head dip down, his mouth move to her neck.

"Why do you get to stay here?" she asked him.

"Melissa knows my mother," he said, his voice muffled against her skin. "They were old friends in college."

There were two cats that he fed, he told her. And he watered the plants. On Tuesdays a maid came to clean. In the summer, there was a gardener who came as well. His hands slid up and down her arms as he talked. She watched the snow make its pile on the porch rails. She shrugged his hands off and stepped away. "So, where are you from?" she asked him.

She saw the look in his face—a flash of something, irritation, then acceptance. He stepped back, too, and told her he was from Baton Rouge. He hated the cold. He could never get warm, he said.

"I can see that," she said. "Look how you're all bundled up."

"My name is Joseph," he said. "Since I'm filling you in on things." He took it in stride, as if the discussion was provisional.

"Well, you know my name," she said.

He gave her a look. "We can stop that now," he said.

He seemed uncomfortable. His eyes wouldn't meet hers. She wondered again if there might have been a Katie Beauchamp, if he had admitted this foolishly, and then needed to hide his vulnerability. Men were like that, she knew. Her own husband had once told her he'd been in love with another girl. She was older than Annie, and had a child already from a previous boyfriend, and he'd been in love with the child, too, he'd said. They'd lived together in Marathon, and when the girl left him he was crazy for a while—he couldn't work, or sleep. "Everything was flipped on end," he said. He and Annie were sitting in his car with the heater on when he told her. It was fall, and the leaves blew across the windshield. She'd started her senior year. She had just kissed him, and he had broken away to tell her this story, as a kind of warning. He had been a machinist then, on his lunch break.

He had a stutter, and a head of thick hair that curled over his work shirt's collar. Annie didn't know him very well, but she knew of him. He had been a few years ahead of her in high school, a boy who drank to erase his stutter, who tried to prove himself by driving along nighttime roads with his headlights off. His story about the girl had produced the opposite effect on Annie, who liked the idea of his passionate intensity. When she got pregnant, she was confident she had won it for herself. But she came to learn he had continued to love the other girl, and simply kept quiet about it. Annie had to deal with his frustration, his moody silences, his dreams about someone else. Some days, she thought she would tell him what she knew, but then she realized he might leave her, and she saw her future—alone and struggling with a child, working and paying bills, and she decided against it. Best to play the game the way they laid it out, she thought. She glanced at Joseph, standing by the glass doors

"My name is Annie," she said. She moved over to the cabinets. "I know how to make hot cocoa."

The first cabinet she opened was filled with liquor. Joseph looked over his shoulder, and chuckled. "That might be better."

Annie reached up and grabbed a bottle by the neck. "What about this?"

Joseph stepped beside her and read the label: Pierre Ferrand 1962. "Perfect," he said.

She put the bottle on the counter. "But what is it?"

Joseph found two bell-shaped glasses. He opened the bottle and sniffed it, and then shrugged, and filled each glass halfway. "Smells good. Like brandy."

"Well, it's a pretty color," she said. She held the glass he handed her up to the light. Joseph took a sip from his. He watched her, waiting.

"You *drink* it, Annie," he said.

She rolled her eyes at him. "What's it taste like?"

"Try it and see."

She thought it would taste like its color—burnt sugar, and it did, at first. But then it was more like raisins, and sweet oranges. It reminded her of fall leaves, still wet and vivid and pliable, littering the ground after rain. She didn't say any of this to him. Things didn't taste like colors, her husband had told her once. Joseph asked if she wanted to sit in the living room, and so they carried their glasses in there and sat down on the couch. The living room was darker than the kitchen. There was a television, hidden away inside another set of cabinets, but neither of them wanted to turn it on. Annie asked him about the professor, and Joseph told a scandalous story about her.

"I don't blame the husband for giving her the boat," she said. "So, are you her next conquest?"

They drank their brandy in long swallows. He had already retrieved the bottle from the kitchen and refilled their glasses.

"Oh, no," he said. He laughed, quietly, shaking his head. He looked down at the carpet. The brandy swirled in his glass.

"But you thought about it, didn't you?"

"I'm thinking about it now that you mention it," he said. He looked back up at her. "No, no way."

"Why not?" she asked. "What would stop you?"

Joseph took a large swallow of brandy. His smile faded. He picked up the bottle and held it up, assessing the level of the liquid. "We're drinking a lot of this," he said.

It was hot in the room. His face was flushed.

"You should take off your sweater," she told him.

She had not thought about her baby waking up, wanting her bottle, until just then. She had put it out of her mind to avoid the guilt. Her husband would have made some calls now, to her mother, a few of her friends, inquiring about her. He would be almost worried, but not quite. She had never left him with the baby before. She was the one who dabbed alcohol on the cord stump, changed her diapers, warm with shit. Only she knew how to wrap her in the blanket to contain her helpless flailing. Annie imagined her daughter's awakening cry. Her husband would have to figure out how to warm the bottle in a pan on the stove. He'd seen her do it before. She felt assured that he would work it all out. But still, she felt the surge of silent disappointment in herself. She wondered if her daughter would notice she was gone. Would there be a time of waiting, and sadness, and then forgetting?

When Annie was in high school her best friend disappeared. Susanna had been home alone, her parents and little brother gone on a ski vacation. Annie had stayed there with her the night before, and then Annie's mother had picked her up for church the next morning. Susanna was a cheerleader. Since they'd been little they'd gone out into Susanna's backyard and Annie would practice her twirling, and Susanna would do her backflips and aerial cartwheels. In the fall they'd wear their sweatpants with "Cheer" written on the butt. They'd rake paths in the leaves like runways, and there'd be sounds of wild turkeys in the woods behind the house. In spring, the mud oozed between Susanna's fingers. The crocuses came up around the cellar door. Annie would wear Susanna's brother's boots. The baton would glimmer against the new sun and the pale sky. Summers they'd spend more time in the pool in their bikinis, or sunbathing with their tops' ties undone. It was winter when Susanna was kidnapped. The night before, she and Annie had taken her father's beer from the cellar refrigerator and gotten drunk. They'd gone out into the snow in the backyard and done their tricks—falling and laughing, the snow cushioning their mistakes. Annie had thrown the baton up and dented the house's siding. They'd laughed so hard they wet their pants. They'd lain in the snow under the house's floodlights making angels.

Joseph slipped the sweater over his head. It left his hair ruffled. The high color remained on his cheeks. He wore a long-sleeved shirt underneath. He was slighter than Annie had believed him to be under the layers of his clothes. She smiled at him. She wondered if he would lean over and try to kiss her.

"Well, what about her lover?" Joseph asked. He was still talking about the professor and the student she had living with her. He held his glass up and gestured with it while he talked.

Annie shrugged. "Oh, what about him?"

"I think he's a good guy. It would be ungentlemanly of me."

Annie gave him a look. She'd left her ring in the little dish by her sink. Before she'd gone to Wegman's she'd washed out bottles, and her ring always caught in the bottle's mouth and slipped off. Joseph looked back at her with his red cheeks, and his glassy eyes.

"What?" he said. "I'm serious."

And she believed he was. "I thought maybe you were being true to Katie Beauchamp."

Joseph stilled. She heard him breathe in slowly, and exhale. He set the glass down on the coffee table, leaned forward and placed his elbows on his knees and did not look at her. Annie wondered if this was a tactic to arouse her pity. But then he turned, and shook his head at her, slowly, his eyes quizzical.

"You're still on that," he said, laughing. She saw that she confused him. His gaze settled on the bell-shaped glass of brandy.

"Maybe we've had too much to drink," she said.

Joseph held the bottle eye-level again. Annie rose from the couch and almost toppled back. She banged her shin against the coffee table. He reached up and grabbed her arm. "Steady now," he said.

"Let's go outside," she said.

Joseph nodded, considering. "A walk, sure."

They went into the kitchen and put on their coats. Joseph struggled to open the sliding glass door. The snow lay against it, a good eight inches, but finally it slid on its runner, and they stepped out into the snow on the porch. Annie noticed he'd kept the bottle of brandy. He saw her glance, and grinned. "It's bitter cold out here," he said. He tried to stuff the bottle in his peacoat pocket, but it wouldn't fit. Annie took it from him and put it in hers. Joseph slid the door shut behind them. Inside the house looked like a photograph of a warm, safe place. Outside, the wind had picked up, and the snow fell sharper on her face. They tromped down the deck steps and into the backyard.

"Now, right here," Joseph said, gesturing with his arm, "is a long hedge of peonies."

"Peonies?" Annie felt the weight of the brandy bottle against her hip.

"You know, those flowers with the big heads, lots of petals? They're all pink, these."

Annie heard the words slur beneath the southern drawl. She thought of flowers with heavy, nodding heads weighing down their stems.

"This lawn is green, and rolling. It's like a damn golf course, I tell you."

Annie looked out. Her face stung with cold. "I see that," she said.

They walked across the lawn, and Joseph told her about the games of croquet.

"We'd play until dark," he said. "Until we couldn't see the balls in the grass anymore. One night the lightning bugs swarmed and we were surrounded by little flying lights."

They had walked a distance from the house, up onto a rise, and were looking down into someone else's wide backyard. The neighbor's house sat at the bottom of the hill, the lights glowing from one or two rooms.

"So who were you with last summer?" Annie asked him.

In the house below them she could see two people moving around in the kitchen, a woman and a man, talking. Joseph didn't look at her.

"Oh, just a friend," he said.

She thought how the man and the woman might be Joseph and herself. She tried to imagine what the two people might have to talk about. She and her husband discussed bills, and the people who came into Clark's, and the baby's needs. Her husband talked about television shows, and movies, and the lives of the actors who played in them. Sometimes, they went a whole day and didn't talk at all. Beside her, Joseph stilled, watching the scene below them, too. She didn't know what he thought as he looked.

"A woman friend, right?" Annie said.

"It's getting late," was all he said.

They walked back through the snow to the professor's house, and up onto the deck. Joseph could not get the sliding door open.

"It's frozen shut maybe," he said. He would go around to try the front, but he didn't have the key, and he doubted he left it open. Annie watched him disappear around the house. In a moment he was back to try the sliding door again. The warm kitchen mocked them through the glass. One of the cats came up and rubbed against the door. They could hear her meowing. Annie began to laugh. Joseph leaned all of his weight against the handle, and collapsed, laughing too, into the snow.

"It won't budge," he said.

Annie stepped off the porch. The snow was still falling, but under the stand of pine the ground showed a knot of roots, and a bed of straw-colored needles. The boat rested serenely on its trailer. "We need some shelter," she called to him. There was a ladder hung from the Bertram's side. "What about the boat? Can we get in it?"

Joseph shook his head at her in disbelief. "No, we can't get *in* it."

But Annie was already trudging over. She took hold of the ladder and pulled herself up. She unclipped the tarp and drew it back. Underneath the deck of the boat was as clean and white as the snow outside. She saw a doorway that led to a cabin. It was quiet, the sound from outside muffled, and she put a leg over and slid down. The brandy bottle made a clumping noise. In a moment, Joseph was there, too, and he pulled himself over the edge and sat down on the deck. He replaced the tarp as best he could. They smelled varnish, and a faint, salty scent.

"It's like being at sea," Annie said, bracing herself against a rolling feeling.

Joseph slit his eyes at her. "You're drunk."

He stood up, bent at the waist, and walked over to the cabin door. Annie followed him down into the berth. There was a small counter and a sink, and a table with cushioned benches, and another door that Joseph opened that led to the sleeping quarters. Annie pulled the brandy out of her pocket. She set it down hard on the table. Joseph came over and sat on one of the benches.

"I can't believe this happened," he said.

Annie sat down across from him. She kept her hand on the neck of the bottle so she wouldn't fall over. The cabin was dark and close and almost warm. Joseph leaned back against the seat and his legs bumped hers under the table.

Joseph shook his head. "If I could get some heat on that door, I could melt the ice."

"It's fine in here," she said. She unzipped her coat. She uncorked the brandy and took a sip.

"You'd better go easy on that," Joseph said.

She slid the bottle over to him. "Someone is sobering up."

Joseph shook his head at her. He took the bottle in his hands, but he didn't drink from it. He hummed a song under his breath, a popular one her husband would know the name of, and Annie remembered the feeling she'd had in the Wegman's parking lot—the sense of things dropping into place, like the coins in the sorter she'd had as a child. She remembered that on the day Susanna disappeared she'd gone home after church and called her later that afternoon and the phone had rung busy. She had thought, fleetingly, that she should go over, but then the feeling faded, and she did not. Susanna's parents were returning that night. The next day Susanna didn't come to school, and Annie thought she was sick, or skipping. Later, in the newspaper, it said that there were *signs of struggle.* Annie had tried to imagine what these might be—the hall table overturned, the plates on which they'd eaten breakfast shattered on the kitchen floor? It had been the neighbor who took her, a single man with thinning hair she and Susanna had always called Lonesome Ricky. He wore silk dress shirts and polyester slacks and aviator-style glasses. When he pulled his car into the driveway Annie used to peek out of Susanna's bedroom window and say, "Lonesome Ricky's brought home a lady," or "Lonesome Ricky has his dancing shoes on," and Susanna would shriek with laughter, and leap up to look out, half-believing her. They hadn't known that he was watching them in the yard the night before, that he had been watching them for years. But even now, Annie believed she'd always known it. Hadn't they sensed someone watching? Hadn't they desired it, even?

"Your shirt is cute," Joseph said.

Susanna and Annie had always shared clothes. It had been perfectly normal while she was alive. But during those weeks when they waited for her to be found, after they knew she was dead, and who had done it, after the funeral, wearing her clothes had seemed, to everyone but Annie, an aberration.

"It's a dead girl's shirt," she told Joseph now. She watched him. He didn't say anything. He took the cork from the brandy and tipped it back against his lips. He kept his eyes on her. Then he lowered the bottle.

"There isn't a dead girlfriend," he said, his voice tight. "I promise I made that up."

He held up his hand, making the Boy Scout pledge. But Annie saw that his eyes flitted away from hers, briefly, hiding what they'd shown her before, in the parking lot, in the kitchen.

"Well, I'm not making it up," she said, slowly, mimicking his southern accent.

He looked down at his hand on the tabletop. He didn't laugh. "You got me," he said. When he finally glanced up at her he looked as if he had tasted something awful.

He drank from the bottle again. His movements were clumsy, and Annie saw everything around her sharpen—the table's edge, the folds of her jacket sleeve, the bottle's lip. He tipped his chin toward her T-shirt.

"How'd she die?"

Annie felt her heart beat light and fast at the base of her throat. Joseph looked at her, waiting, his eyes sad, and remorseful. She wasn't sure who he saw when he looked at her now, and she felt sorry she'd played along. She could not be Katie Beauchamp. After she'd learned the details of Susanna's death Annie would imagine how it might have been if she'd gone over to her friend's house that afternoon and been taken as well, the two of them bound with duct tape in the trunk of Lonesome Ricky's rusted Grand Prix.

Once, Annie had convinced Susanna to sneak into the drive-in with her, hiding in Annie's boyfriend's trunk. His car had been his father's, a big sedan, and they'd fit easily curled alongside each other. They hadn't been afraid, feeling the potholes of a familiar road, knowing that beyond the metal trunk lid lay the summer night sky, dotted with stars. They could hear their boyfriends' voices, and they'd talked and laughed at themselves the entire ride, until the boys called out that they'd reached the drive-in entrance, and then they were quiet so they wouldn't get caught.

Joseph looked at her, his gaze steady. "You can't talk about it," he said. His knees pressed hers under the table. The snow tapped against the portholes.

In Lonesome Ricky's trunk Susanna's hair would smell of her shampoo, and her skin like the lotion they bought that weekend at the mall, all of her plans waylaid for this unforeseen moment—the outfit left hanging on her closet door knob, the biology book opened to the assigned page on her bed. Their mouths sealed, they could not speak. The trunk would have been cold, the exhaust leaking in through the rusted holes, and they might have pressed their bodies close for warmth, and heard the tires hum, and Lonesome Ricky's radio playing old disco, his voice singing along. Annie would not imagine any further. From this point she was always, magically, outside of the car, watching it wind along a road through bare trees and white snow, and only the deer, poised on the edge of the woods, witnessed what came after.

Now, outside of the boat's hull a car horn sounded, and then, clearly, one of Joseph's friends called out, his voice carrying around the side of the house from the driveway. Annie remembered her car was still there, that her keys were in her jacket pocket. At the little house Annie and her husband rented, miles of narrow-ribboned, snow-covered asphalt away, her infant daughter cried, her tiny face red, her small hands balled at the end of her gown's sleeves. She did not cry for Annie, or for anything she could understand, but for the sake of crying, an urge. Annie read that in a book she'd been given by one of her high school friends at the baby shower her mother hosted. All of the cheerleaders and twirlers had sat in a circle, while Annie in her bulky body tore pastel-colored paper from gifts she could not, at the time, fathom having a need for.

Joseph took one of her hands in his, carefully. "I don't think we can die in a yacht in a snowstorm," he said, his voice low.

Through the portholes the sky was gray with burden, and out of it the snow tumbled, delicate and dizzying. Annie heard his friend call out again, the voice closer now, rounding the side of the house, and she looked at Joseph, waiting for him to respond. He raised a finger to her lips. He slid his hand down around her neck, and pressed his thumb to the base of her throat. The things she hadn't said swelled up now, under the pressure of his thumb. She leaned forward until their mouths touched, the words readying themselves, graceful as breath.

on the lake

It was spring when his grandmother died, the funeral nearly an hour's drive in the light rain, with trees budding bright against their wet black limbs all along Route 44, through Avon, Canton, and New Hartford, and Paul insisting we listen to Clapton, and his sister telling childhood stories of their father, who died five years before in a murder-suicide involving his second wife. I wore a gray wool skirt and the light rain beaded up on the front of it. The waistband was too tight, and I worried about being pregnant, alternately believing and disbelieving it. We went first to the funeral home, where I sat in a semicircle of folding chairs with his family, and people came and cried on me. My hands were taken and enfolded in the small, dry, withered hands of old women, the fleshy hands of middle-aged men, who leaned their faces close to mine, showing me their moles, and cracked lips. "You poor, poor thing," they said. I didn't know any of them, and their tears wet the shoulder of my blouse, the lank strands of my hair. I had only met Paul's grandmother once, when he took me to her house for dinner, and she sat tired and depleted in a chair at the table, watching everyone eat the food she'd spent all day preparing—steaming plates of gnocchi alla sorrentina. I remembered her gray hair looking like she set it the night before in pink foam rollers, her quick, assessing eyes, her ashen face. Lying out she looked almost the same, save for the eyes, which were closed, and unable to judge me where I stood, young and alive, peering into her casket. Hers was the first dead body I ever saw.

Paul knew I didn't want to go, that I did it for him. I made him understand this the day before in his basement bedroom. It had already begun to rain and the new spring grass grew against the window and gave the room a greenish tinge. He had asked me to come over on my lunch break to have sex. He didn't say as much, but that was all we did together at the time, and I didn't mind the sex simply because I understood he wanted it with me, and no one else. There was something to that, I thought. I took my clothes off and folded each piece and set everything on the top of his bureau. I stood on the floor's cold cement. He lay on the bed watching me.

"I can't really see it," he said. He looked at my stomach, his eyes squinched.

I put both of my hands there. "It would only be two months."

I had already told him that I wouldn't have it, but every day or so he tried to change my mind. I found this endearing. He was still not working from his motorcycle accident and he spent most of his day on painkillers in his basement room, watching television. People came by in the evenings to visit him. I don't think he ever really got dressed. He was able to climb the stairs though, for food, and if he'd backed off the Demerol he might have even been able to work at something, but he knew that, and it made this stretched-out period of recuperation that much more heady. We were both eighteen. His sister, Lena, was two years older, and her room was next door to Paul's, just a small bed pushed up under the basement stairs. She had gotten married after high school and then divorced. Paul's mother told them both they had to sleep in the basement, maybe as a kind of punishment for not making good choices, but I thought it was more likely for not being the kind of children she'd always wanted.

Paul was still very boyish. He grinned a lot and cracked jokes, and people thought he was funny. When I first met him I was a senior, and before we'd had sex we'd stay out all night in his car, just listening to the radio and reading the newspaper under the dim map light. Sometimes, I'd do my homework. We both had that in common, a resistance to going home. Now, he stared at me with heavy-lidded eyes.

"I'm not staying late today," I warned him. I jumped onto the bed and slid on top of him, careful of his left leg. His hands stayed by his sides. He made a kind of grunt, and smiled.

"You got the day off tomorrow, right?" he asked.

I didn't answer. I buried my face against his shoulder. His hands lay inert on the bedcover. "You're going to *do* something, right?" I asked him. He took his time with his hands, the fingers moving in slow motion up the backs of my legs and down again.

"I can't go without you," he said.

"I've never been to a funeral," I told him.

"What are you afraid of?" he said. He laughed then, and I felt his chest move up and down. "There's a party after. We'll see Frank and everyone."

The night I met his grandmother we went out with Paul's cousins to someone's house on Highland Lake, where there was a lot of shag carpeting and a low ceiling and a point in the night where I stopped remembering anything.

"You had fun that night," he said.

"That was different," I told him. I wanted to say there wasn't a body involved, but I didn't. It was the body, really, that frightened me. But he thought I meant the baby.

He was quiet then. His hands fell away.

"You're my *girlfriend,"* he said.

And I guessed I was. I thought how it was almost nice, to belong to someone else. I didn't know if I loved him, but I had found I could pretend I did, easily, and even enjoy my own pretending. I worked in an office complex down the street, and I almost liked that, too—showing up each day at a regular time, wearing a skirt and blouse and nice shoes. I sensed though, even then, that none of this would last, that inside of me existed a moment, timed and inevitable, when I would abandon all of it.

The funeral was in St. Joseph's Church, and the burial in the old cemetery behind it on the hill. The whole thing ended at three o'clock, when the rain stopped and was replaced with a sodden, muggy thickness. The town, a small one surrounding the lake, reached its peak years ago in the manufacture of clock parts. Unlike nearby Riverton, where the Hitchcock Chair Factory was, it was now tired and drained of any real industry. The houses, built along steeply graded roads, seemed forlorn, with their peaked roofs, and mailboxes leaning over the asphalt, and TV antennas dripping and glistening in the weak spring sunlight. I was hot in my skirt. In the church I'd held onto my Mass card so tightly it had gotten damp. I had forgotten when to kneel and stand. I felt vacant and unforgiven after, though I'd said my own confession and penance sitting there in the pew. I had been too long sealed off in Paul's subterranean room.

During the service Lena's mascara ran. Now, she sniffled behind the wheel of the car. Paul never cried. He kept his face down, and there were creases between his eyes, as if he pinched everything in. It was seductive, all of this sorrow. I had never felt so joined in mutual sadness. Even Clapton sang mournfully from the car stereo.

"Holy shit, turn that off already," Lena shrieked. She was a tiny woman with wild dark hair. Paul looked entirely different, pale, freckled, and blue-eyed. His mother told me, once, as we drank wine out by her newly constructed concrete pool, that when they brought Paul to her as a newborn she'd insisted he wasn't hers. She sipped her wine and laughed. Her name was Lisanne. Her face was small, surrounded by the same wild hair as her daughter. I didn't tell her that except for the hair and the coloring she and Paul looked exactly alike. This was just after the accident last summer, when they thought he wouldn't make it, and then he did. Paul was still in the hospital. She invited me to her house for dinner, and we sat outside by her pool, the grass newly planted around its perimeter, and pots of pansies nodding and fluttering. I had never had wine with an adult before. Usually, we stole bottles from our parents and drank them out in the woods, passing the bottle back and forth. That evening, we drank from Lisanne's old wedding crystal. It was the glasses that prompted her to reminisce about Paul's father. She divorced him when Paul was a toddler. Back then, she told me, it wasn't very acceptable.

"I had to move in with my mother," she said. "I was about your age, with these two kids. But anything was better than the alternative."

She shook her head, slowly, from side to side. I could tell she'd had a lot to drink, but I liked her, and it only made her nicer, more accessible. She told me how Paul's father used to come home at night and wake her up and accuse her of sleeping with someone else.

"And the look on his face," she said. She widened her eyes. "If I wore lipstick, he asked me who I was wearing it for. He was a crazy man. Well, obviously. Thank God I left when I did."

I didn't ask many questions then. It was probably a failing of mine, this refusal to inquire further. She had assumed I knew the story, but of course at the time I did not. Paul never talked about his father. He did let me take a sport coat, a wide-wale green corduroy I found in his basement closet, which I wore that whole fall and winter, but I never asked whom it belonged to. And then one night when Paul had fallen asleep I heard Lena come in, and I went out to sit with her on her bed. Sometimes she'd mentioned things, like her half-brother, who was six years old, and his aunt and uncle, who were raising him now, and I'd wonder. That night she had come from spending the day with them and she was subdued and tired from the drive, but she wanted to talk, she said, so I sat there on the edge of her bed. It was winter, and the furnace kept kicking on. In the little laundry room I could see Lisanne's bras and panties swaying on a line.

"I just don't know how he could do it," she said. She looked up at me, her hair spread out on her pillow. "He was my father, and I still can't believe it."

I smiled, weakly, hoping to seem comforting.

"He doesn't ever talk about it, does he?" she asked me, her eyes moving to Paul's closed bedroom door. I shook my head, slowly, realizing she would now tell me the story. Some things I'd rather not have known, and this was one of them.

As we drove to Paul and Lena's grandmother's house, up and down the little paved hills toward the lake, Lena pointed out the house where her father last lived, tapping her nail on the window glass as we passed, and it was one of the older houses, with a front porch where a family might have sat on summer evenings and listened to the crickets, or talked about their day at work, or watched spring rain dampen and brighten their lawn, and yet all I could imagine was some blood-spattered wood-paneled family room, with lamps overturned onto predictable shag carpeting, and a one-year old asleep in a back bedroom.

The grandmother's house, I remembered, was a cottage on stilts. There'd been a dock, and a boat tied up. Their grandfather had died years before. Everyone assumed the house would be willed to the daughter, their aunt, who lived nearby in town. But the news had come, before the funeral, that the grandmother had wanted the house to go to her son, and after his death, one she always had trouble accepting, she had given it to the next male descendant. So, the house went to Paul. No one seemed to be angry, or question it.

"Oh, the house, the house," they all said, patting him on the back. Their eyes were wet, their noses red. Paul shrugged. What did he want with his dead grandmother's house? he said in the car. Lena hit him when he said it, and he cringed.

"Daddy grew up in that house," she said.

Paul had the window down and he lit a cigarette, and the ash blew into the backseat onto my lap. Normally, he was only quiet when he couldn't think of something funny to say. I saw him slump toward the passenger door, and he rode that way until we reached the house, a tiny place painted dark green with white trim. It had a small scraggly hedge and a gravel driveway that curved through a meadow of sorts that used to be the front lawn, blooming with tiny violet and white flowers. Two of the shutters were missing. The front door was propped open and the dark interior was lit yellow from a living room lamp. Overhead the sky was white with clouds. "This is a cute house," I said, and both of them ignored me. Around us came the sound of car doors closing, one after the other.

We filed inside with everyone else. It smelled of basil and wet metal window screens and, faintly, of closed off cedar closets. Others had already arrived, and they pushed in close, and some, including Paul and I, squeezed past to spill out onto the deck in back and the dock that extended over the lake, its surface glassy and black. Near the muddy shore little yellow buttercups bloomed in the grasses. Paul looked out over the water. He wore his heavy-framed sunglasses and smoked another cigarette. I knew he'd taken more than his usual dose of pills, that he had brought extra in a baggy in his pants pocket. He was too quiet, too removed. We sat down onto a sofa glider, its vinyl cushion covered with a mildewed print of flowers. Paul put his arm across my shoulders and leaned into my blouse. My legs were damp under my wool skirt. I felt the wearying ache in my abdomen that had lately begun to make me uncomfortable, one I could not attribute to the tight skirt. The idea of a baby stretching out its forming limbs was troubling, and I tried my hardest not to imagine it. Lena flitted from group to group, enveloped by the men's shirtsleeves, the women's long, veiny arms and jangling bracelets. We sat apart from everyone, pushing the sofa glider back and forth on its runners, making a rusty squeak.

Occasionally Lena brought someone over to us, and Paul would glance up and nod and listen to their reverie about how his grandfather was the first on the lake to purchase lightning rods for the house, or how his grandmother knew all the words to every song of Rogers and Hammerstein's *My Fair Lady.* One of the aunts brought us vodka tonics with small pieces of floating limes. I sipped mine, the glass smelling of the aging kitchen shelf paper. Then Lena came back around with another old man on her arm.

"This is Mr. Capra," she said. "The neighbor."

The man, balding, wearing an ill-fitting brown suit, began his story. I felt Paul's inward groan.

"Every Friday after school your father would mow the lawn down short as could be for the bocce games. He'd wear a white T-shirt and his school slacks, a slim, good-looking boy."

Mr. Capra's drink sloshed a little as he spoke. Lena grinned, holding his arm.

"Everyone from the neighborhood played," she said.

"Oh it was a variety of people," the man continued. "Your father was the champ."

Paul's smile was too wide. "Oh yessiree," he said.

I saw the man's wistful expression darken. Lena gave Paul a sharp glance and led Mr. Capra away. I got up to use the bathroom and when I got back Paul handed me my glass. "Drink up," he said. He slumped over and closed his eyes. I nudged him with my elbow.

"Don't go to sleep."

The sun set, a branching of light bands across the black water. I drank my drink. The air was still thick and buzzing now with newborn flies. No one seemed to pay any attention to me, and then a man approached, one I'd heard everyone call Sammy, whose shirt, marked with sweat, seemed unbearably tight across his chest.

"What do you want to eat, sweetheart?" he asked me. He squatted down in front of me. His eyes were earnest and sweet. He couldn't convince me to eat anything. I wasn't feeling well, I said. Paul had fallen asleep beside me and no one seemed to think it strange. Sammy shifted his weight to stand. He put one of his big hands on my knee, under the hem of my skirt, and squeezed it, and I couldn't tell if he was still kind, or if there was something else he wanted me to understand. He stepped away, and I watched his glowing shirt move through the dusk into the house. I shoved Paul off of my shoulder, and he sat upright. His eyes remained closed.

"Where'd you go?" he asked. The words slurred.

"I want to change my clothes," I told him. "I'm sweaty."

He stood up then, his bad leg buckling, and took my hand, and we threaded our way back inside, through the tiny living room crowded with people, photos of the dead relatives, crocheted doilies, and overflowing ceramic ashtrays, through the kitchen with its table of foil-covered dishes, to a bedroom at the back of the house. The cool darkness smelled of lilac and talcum. The bed had a satiny green cover. Paul opened the bureau drawers, one at a time, and sorted through the contents.

"I'm not wearing your grandmother's clothes," I said.

On the wall hung a crucifix, and stuck into the rim of the bureau mirror were a dozen Mass cards, all with the same flowery script, and various aspects of Jesus' face. "Who will wear them?" he asked me. "My aunt is too fat."

He held up a pair of khaki Bermuda shorts. "We'll just give this stuff away," he said. "And then you can buy it for a quarter at the Goodwill store." He tossed the shorts onto the bed, and dug around some more until he found a pink souvenir T-shirt from Hawaii.

"Hey," he said. "I gave this to her."

We both looked at the T-shirt, creased from its long stay in the drawer.

He threw it down on the bed with the shorts. Then he stood in front of me and untucked my blouse. I tried to stop him, but he grabbed my hands and set them aside and I let them dangle, loose and surrendered. Then he undid the buttons, his fingers thick and awkward. The room was dim, and he missed one, so that when he went to take the blouse off the button ripped from the shirt. It flew across the room and pinged against something. "Jesus," I said.

Paul chuckled. "He's all around you."

Beyond the room we heard the voices of people pouring drinks in the kitchen, the Formica counter with its myriad of bottles now a makeshift bar. The voices were garrulous and loud, often full of laughter, lured from their sadness by the liquor. They came into the room, and left the room, like the noise of humming insects. Paul unzipped my skirt and we watched it slip to the floor. I stepped out of it in my pumps.

"What about shoes?" I asked.

But he leaned in with his mouth and the room, with its shadows, and its shiny satin quilt, seemed to drop away like the sides of a magician's box. I felt his mouth slide down my neck to my breasts. I imagined that beneath the wooden floorboards the lake water slapped against the house's pilings, the fish slunk in the murk, shrewd and ancient.

"You spiked my drink," I said. The voices in the house, on the deck, became a ringing of bells. My own voice was far off, somewhere below that sound. I thought it was funny that he had done this to me. We kissed for a very long time. We fell back onto the bed. But, it was as if we had forgotten what else we might be doing. The kissing seemed to be all we could manage, and it went on and on and I wanted it to stop. I felt a bit panicked that someone would come in, and worse than their recognizing me in his grandmother's clothes was the worry that I would be caught naked in her bed.

"This is my bedroom now," he said. "If I want, this will be my bed."

We looked at each other, our faces barely readable in the dark.

"If I want, I can raise a whole little family here," he said.

"One day, maybe you can."

Outside on the deck the voices had diminished, and we heard the sputtering sound of a boat's motor.

"It's Frank, Paul said.

He sat up and told me to dress. "I want to take the boat out," he said. He left me in the room, in the dark. The satin bedcover slid against my skin. I wouldn't let myself think about what he had said about the house, and the family. He hadn't really meant it, anyway. I sat up, slowly, and found the clothes at the foot of the bed. The shorts hung along my hips, and their looseness was comforting. The T-shirt smelled of the little sachets his grandmother kept in the drawers. I found a small lamp on the bedside table, and I pulled open the closet door to look at the shoes. There were some navy blue sneakers new in the box, and though they were a half-size too small, I put them on. I went out through the kitchen to the back deck. A group gathered at the end of the dock where a white motorboat churned up the lake. Paul was there, waiting. He grabbed my arm and pulled me in.

"Remember my wife?" he said. Frank, a burly teenager with black eyes raised an eyebrow. It was cool now near the water. The lake smelled of algae, and I thought I heard the mud sucking at the pilings. I found it difficult to stand upright. I kept listing against Paul's arm. Around us the cousins, all girls, seemed to retreat, their long hair blowing, their arms around their waists, hiding their breasts.

"Nice shoes," Frank said. I remembered then that he was sarcastic and hard to like. It was terrible to be wearing their dead grandmother's clothes.

"Paul gave them to me," I said. I wiggled my toes against the canvas.

Paul looked down, confused. Then he laughed. He tipped his head all the way back and teetered on his bad leg toward the edge of the dock. Frank reached forward and grabbed the front of his shirt. "Oh, man," he said, clucking his tongue. He looked at us for a few long moments. "I can't take you two out," he said.

"What are you talking about?" Paul said. He stepped forward and pointed his finger at Frank's chest. "I'll take the boat myself."

"I don't really want to go," I said. I held onto Paul's hand, but he shrugged my hand away. I wanted to go back to the bed in the cool, dry air and lie down. Paul limped over to the side of the boat and swung a leg in, and Frank had no choice but to join him. I stood on the dock with the remaining female cousins, all dark-eyed, with bright mouths, like gypsies.

"What about the wife?" Frank said, and Paul told him to bring me onboard. He was happy now that he'd gotten his way. I saw the lit end of his cigarette, a tiny beacon, and so I allowed myself to be helped into the boat. Frank gripped my wrist, and I leaned into his chest. His shirtfront smelled of cologne and I wondered if he had a girlfriend, and if he'd graduated high school yet, and a few other things that occurred to me being up against him. I think he wondered, too, because he pushed me, roughly, into the remaining seat and ran his hands through his dark hair before making his announcement.

"You pretty much know," he said, "that if one of you goes over in the dark you can forget about being saved."

I laughed, a small, childish sound that surprised me, and he looked at me, his eyebrows drawn together. I felt a little guilty about making him be the parent. His cousins threw the lines into the boat, and Frank moved quickly, gathering them and positioning himself behind the wheel. We moved away from the dock slowly, and then he eased the throttle and we moved faster over the water, which parted greenish black and sprayed up along the sides. The wind filled my nose and mouth. I felt I couldn't catch my breath. I looked over at Paul, but I couldn't see much with my hair flying over my face. Frank stood, his own hair blown straight back, the wind pulling at his dress shirt like a sail.

I knew, from Lena, that this had been Paul's father's boat, that when they visited him here, before he married his second wife, he would take them out for rides. Lena said she went only twice. She was afraid, she said. Her father went too fast. He stopped at the center of the lake and let the boat roll and dip, and told them he ran out of gas. Once, he slipped off the bow and hid from them in the water, and they had panicked, thinking he had drowned. She told me all of this the last time we were here, when Paul had wished he could take out the boat. But it was winter, and the docks along the lakeshore shone with colored Christmas lights, and the lake was frozen over. Paul had still been using crutches at the time, and he was in more pain, but he hadn't yet started abusing the painkillers and he had been different, softer and thoughtful. I had never been with anyone who almost died before, and during that time, while I waited to hear and cried for him in my bedroom, I'd felt chosen, and special, and obligated.

I felt none of that now. The black lake and the dark, moonless night blended. I saw the rim of lake house lights, blinking and distant. Paul sat with his arm thrown over the seat back, watching me. I didn't know what he wanted anymore. Frank slowed the boat and we went along, closer to one of the docks. This was his friend's house, the place where we had the party months ago. Frank hit the horn, and a door opened, and a boy sauntered out along the dock in what looked like pajama bottoms and no shirt.

"What?" he called, throwing his arms up.

"I've got Paulie and his *wife,"* Frank said.

The boy seemed familiar—the set of his bony shoulders, the sound of his voice. I remembered then that he and I had gone into a bathroom together in the house behind him. There had been a Virgin Mary nightlight and a little dish of scented soaps. The sink was pale blue porcelain with a rusty mark where the water dripped. I had kissed him, and maybe more had happened, but I didn't want to remember it now. The boy on the dock laughed. His voice was musical off the lake.

"Do they want to use the bathroom?" he asked.

Paul snorted. He looked at me. "Do you?"

You never knew what he was thinking. You wanted to believe you did, and for a while that would work. The night became sharp and fixed with stars. I glanced at Frank, and he was looking down at his shoes.

"No?" Paul asked. He was grinning, widely, unnaturally. I couldn't imagine when he found out, maybe the next morning when I woke him up from the couch, or the day after that, or just now. There was no real culpability. It didn't matter what I'd done if he didn't care. I listened to the boat's motor rumble. And then Frank waved an arm and turned the boat around. The lights of the houses grew small and wavering. Paul wanted Frank to stop out on the center of the lake. We bobbed there on the surface, the air stilled and silent. A dog's bark came across the water.

"We should take her to Hippie Hollow," Paul said. Frank smiled. He pulled out a cigarette and offered us each one from his pack. Then he lit them for us, the lighter hot near my face. I didn't want to smoke, but I had nothing to do with my hands.

"What is that?" I asked. Neither of them looked at me.

When Paul wouldn't answer Frank did. "It's the nude beach," he said. "On the other side of the lake."

I didn't know what to say. "Old people go there mostly," Frank said. He shrugged, and I think he felt a little sorry for me.

"This is my boat now," Paul said.

"It was always yours," Frank said. He shook his head. "You just never wanted it."

Paul smoked quietly. "I wonder why."

The boat bobbled and dipped. The water sloshed against its sides.

"It's an old one, a pain to keep up," Frank told him.

"A lot of things I don't understand," Paul said. "And then some, well, suddenly I do." He nodded his head. He stood, unsteadily, and flicked his cigarette overboard. Frank turned back to the wheel and we started off again. I watched Paul go to the side and sit on the edge. I can't say if I saw his face or his expression in the dark, just the slow, purposeful leaning back, and his body rolling off. I screamed his name. Frank immediately slowed, as if he knew without looking. He handed me a flashlight and idled low, turning the boat around. The flashlight's beam trembled over the surface, choppy from the wake. We saw him within minutes, heard his arms beating against the water. Frank swore at him over the side. I heard the tension and fear in his voice, and I stayed back and did as I was told: hold the wheel right, keep the throttle low. Frank took off his shirt and went in to get him. I lost sight of them for a moment and my heart whipped up in my chest, and then Frank's arm hooked over the side. There was a ski platform on back, and he brought Paul around and dragged him up on that.

They got back into the boat and lay out on the deck and their bodies steamed. Paul was laughing. He pulled himself upright, his clothes sodden with lake water. He took out his wet cigarettes and put one in his mouth and tried to light it, the water dripping from his shirtsleeve, the flame jumping up and down from his laughing. I felt the cramps in my abdomen sharpen and I put my shaking hands there, as if they could stop what had already begun to happen. The engine stalled out. Around us the water was an invisible slapping force. No one said anything, and finally Paul stopped laughing, and in the quiet you could hear Frank's heavy, sorrowful sounding breaths.

destiny

Marianne is named after a song by Frankie Valli and the Four Seasons. I named her myself—her father doesn't even know we're alive. He's probably still driving his pearl-white Chevelle down some turnpike every night, plugging in eight-track tapes of the Raspberries, who sing out the open car windows, "Please go all the way," to any teenage girls within earshot.

I've vowed that I will not let Marianne be fooled like I was. I've been trying to set an example—staying chaste, uninvolved—but sometimes I find myself imagining Marianne years from now, at fifteen: brown hair streaming under violet street lights, a silver charm bracelet jingling on her wrist, staring up at someone's face, or at the moon . . . and I ache with jealousy, with a mysterious excitement that has nothing to do with my life in the past. I'm fooling myself, of course. I already know that Marianne is the only thing I can love and not pay for, ultimately, with my soul.

We have lived in Florida for two years—one with James Copper, the makeup instructor I met at modeling school in Massachusetts, and one on our own. I'm still not used to this damp heat, this thick air, but Marianne doesn't care that her clothes stick to her skin. I've even taken her with me, job hunting, in my old Chevy Impala that has no air conditioning. A few months ago, on the way home, the Impala died in the middle of an intersection. Marianne cried, "Go Mommy go," scattering her crayons as she climbed from the backseat to the front to tug on my arm. Other cars screeched and swerved to avoid hitting us, and finally three men in white clothes came from nowhere and pushed the car into a Sears parking lot. It was a hot day and their white shirts were wet. Marianne kissed the top of my arm as we watched the men disappear down the sidewalk, wiping their foreheads with the backs of their hands.

At first, we didn't get out of the car. I was thinking about the photographer I'd just seen, who'd examined my proof sheets with a magnifying glass and said, "There's something about the mouth . . ."—as if it weren't *my* mouth in the picture, as if *I* weren't sitting there on the low couch in front of him, with my knees jutting, pointed and thin, out from under a tight, black skirt. I looked at my mouth in the rearview mirror. Then Marianne whispered something in my ear, pointing to a display of bright metal swing sets assembled on the concrete in front of Sears.

We had to walk home. Heat rose off car bumpers and the glare of sidewalks. Cars flew past and blew the heat up my skirt. *I am not living,* I remember thinking. *The living thing inside of me has left, and I am just a shell of a person walking down a street, holding a little girl whose legs dangle to the knobs of my knees, who takes my face in her two small hands and says, "Ask me 'Who do you love?'* " Her hair was sticking to the side of her face. I pushed her head down on my shoulder and kept walking, past the tire place where the men stopped working to whistle at me. I wanted to scream *These legs hurt* and *There is something about this mouth,* but I didn't. I was a shell of a person. Yet the bones of the child pressed into my arms, warm and real, unbearably small, achingly beautiful.

Finally, we reached our house—almost hidden in the shade of the neighbor's trees—a tiny building with reddish-brown paint peeling off all four walls. The sky hung over our heads, dismal, gray and weighted with rain. Inside, the smell of old wood and mold was familiar, oddly consoling. Milk stood congealed in a bowl outside the backdoor. Marianne brought it in and dumped it in the sink. She was very quiet, staring out the door at the bare backyard, the one lean tree and the railroad track.

"It would fit right there," she said.

I wanted to tell her that those swing sets are cheap, that they have to be cemented into the ground or they come up and tip, that the metal bends and the screws fall out. Instead I said, "I used to have one of those."

"With two swings?" she asked. "With two swings and a slide? Tell me."

So I told her about the swing set in Massachusetts that I got one year for Christmas, all set up in the garage on the gray cement, just like at Sears.

"When are we going there?" she wanted to know. We are always half packed, ready to go somewhere. The living room is lined with cardboard boxes. We just dig things out as we need them: clothes, hairbrushes, electric rollers.

"We've already been there," I began—then stopped, my voice lost under the sudden slap of rain on the roof. I stood at the door and watched it blur weeds and leaves into bright green smears. Behind me, game-show contestants screamed on the television, and Marianne lay curled in a ball on the couch with one finger in her mouth.

For the first two years of Marianne's life we lived with my mother in the house where I grew up. She is a divorced woman possessed by a lingering sadness that makes her mouth sag. The sadness hangs about her body, smelling of Chanel No. 5. In the late afternoon, sitting at the white iron table in the damp shade of the back yard, she drank manhattans from a large tumbler with a red PGA insignia on it. I always thought this glass belonged to my father, a man I created who played golf and wore sweaters that smelled of tobacco. Now I think it could have belonged to some other woman's husband who left it on the counter one day. The neighbors always strolled across our lawn with drinks in their hands. I would hear them below my window while I changed Marianne: low voices laughing, and ice cubes banging against the sides of heavy glasses.

The rain didn't last long. Once it stopped, Marianne and I sat outside in one of the dripping lawn chairs someone had left here long ago. The woven plastic slats are worn through, and sometimes lizards slide out from under the armrests. We just sat and watched the railroad track steam. Our neighbor's trees were dense and shiny with rain, reminding me of my mother's giant, green umbrella and her hallway tile floor that was like ice under my bare feet, even in summer.

My mother loved Marianne. When she kissed her goodnight, she would clutch the crib rail and sway down until her mouth was right by Marianne's tiny ear. Her lipstick brushed Marianne's face and she would whisper to her, sometimes calling her my name by mistake. "I love you, Roxanna," she would say—the only time I have ever heard her say those words. The memory made me uneasy, wavering in and out like the noise of insects in the trees around us. When Marianne insisted that the noise is made by spiders, weaving webs with machines, I couldn't help laughing. She pinched my arm and gritted her teeth. It's all right for her to hate me, I thought. I'm prepared for it. I have secured a soft wall around me, waiting. It is normal: all daughters hate their mothers.

I told this to Janine, my friend from across the street who had joined us in the backyard. She stood in front of me, shaking her head, her hands on her hips.

"Who says?" she wanted to know.

"James Copper," I said.

"Oh," she smiled and rolled her eyes, "the makeup guy. Why would you believe him?"

"Why not?"

Janine looked at me as if she knew something and didn't want to tell.

"You mean you would believe a guy who fed you all that crap about being a model, who carted you all the way to Florida and left you and a two-year-old alone for months at a time in a dumpy apartment?" Her face was flushed and she was waving her hands in the air. "Think about that!" she shouted.

I did. I thought about being in the Impala that my mother bought for me after Marianne was born, about Marianne asleep in the backseat with her legs buried under a pile of my dresses, about me crying and James Copper smoothing my hair and telling me things that I had to believe then—having already driven six hours on the interstate with my mother's swing records from the 1940s stacked on the floor and all my shoes (twenty pairs in brightly colored boxes) wedged in the trunk. Janine would not understand any of it. I looked at her soft, puffy face and furious eyes. I could never tell her about pulling off at a Stuckey's while Marianne slept, how he drove around back and pushed my head down into his lap, stroked my hair and my neck and my back. How I imagined the waitresses in their brown uniforms leaving work, squeaking past the car in their white rubber-soled shoes, wondering: *What is that man doing alone in that car with his head thrown back? Is he dead?*

Janine glared at me as if she wanted to punish me, but then her eyes softened.

She tried to turn away before I could see that she loves me. It was getting dark and she squinted at the empty dirt drive, moved a few steps back so she could see the street.

"Where's your goddamn car?" she asked.

"At Sears," I said. I didn't even look up at her. With Marianne squirming on my lap, I imagined sitting in this spot forever, becoming part of the outdoors with vines in my hair and weeds sprouting from my toes. I was comfortable.

"Even you, Roxanna, have a right to be happy," Janine said quietly.

"I am happy," I said. I closed my eyes and listened for the rustling of stems winding around my ankles. Marianne's legs were making wet marks on my thighs. We wore identical ponytails and I lifted hers, kissed her neck where it was salty, soft. I wanted to cry but decided to hold it in, to wait until it burned in my chest, a sweet pain.

Soon after the car was repaired I took Marianne to the beach.

"Florida is a beautiful place," I told her. "We can be anything we want."

"I want to be a model," she said. She can already put on lipstick expertly, without a mirror.

"Then we need tans," I said. We held hands and smiled, the sand scalding the bottoms of our feet. I had bought Marianne polka-dotted sunglasses and a pair of rubber thongs, but I still couldn't bear to look at her squatting on the bright towel, holding her knees, her tiny bones poking against the white skin of her back.

"Some things," she told me, "aren't very fun, even if they're supposed to be."

Not long after that I found a job through a modeling agency. I've had to work nights, but Janine has been willing to come over and watch Marianne for some time now. Her husband doesn't mind. She makes him dinner and leaves him with it in front of the TV. "Like an animal," she tells me, "only I put it on Corelle instead of in a metal bowl."

She had just arrived last night when my mother called and screamed at me over the phone: "I want my records back, do you hear me!"

"I don't have those anymore," I said, as Marianne swished around the room in one of my full slips, moving to the rhythm of "Love Me or Leave Me." Cicadas whined through the screen door, and the wind was pulling the cream curtains out and back.

"You had no right to do that," my mother cried, so close to hysteria that I hung up on her. Usually she'll just call back the next day and ask for Marianne, angry with me without knowing why.

I left Janine and Marianne and drove to my job at a popular night club. I dance there, in a square cage made of metal bars enameled black, with a Plexiglas floor. I wear costumes that match the theme of the night—Biker Bash, Wild West, Pajama Party. If someone is sick the manager sometimes asks me to waitress. Either way I make money, but I'd rather be behind the bars where no one can touch me. People my own age come to the club, right out of high school with fake IDs—girls in their mother's designer clothes, guys with long hair tied back and wearing shoes of expensive leather. I've gotten to know them. I watch them fall in love with each other. I see who two-times, who lies, which ones to trust. They act out their lives in the club while I dance and watch them. Older men throw money onto the square floor of the cage, and I fold the bills into tiny squares, tucking them in the toes of my patent leather pumps.

This job is only temporary. I don't have any other plans, but I know things will change soon. I felt it last night, driving home at two a.m. with the car windows down, in the way the air moved the hair on my arms. I had to stop at a convenience store to buy cigarettes for Janine, and I saw a man in a green army coat sitting on a duffel bag under the payphone. He looked straight at me, and I was startled by his eyes, the silence of his face like that of a statue. When I came back out, a police car was parked next to mine, and the cop was telling the man to leave, waving his stick in the air while he talked. I opened my car door and the man stood up and looked at me again. I motioned toward him with my hand.

"Let's go," I said. I felt bold and strange. He got in the car, leaving the cop open-mouthed, and we drove away.

His name is Jeffrey. He smells of the outside, of fresh open air.

"I'm nomadic," he told me, laughing quietly.

When we reached my house I went inside alone, gave Janine her cigarettes, and watched her walk home. Then I sneaked Jeffrey in. I showed him Marianne, sleeping in the bedroom. Her body was nearly invisible under the patterned sheet: a small raised spot, a fold that I could flatten with my hand. Jeffrey and I slept without clothes on the prickly material of the secondhand couch. Before dawn he disappeared, and I crept back into the bed I share with Marianne. Her fingers curled around the pale sheet, revealing small crescents of dirt under her fingernails. As I brushed her thin hair from her face my hand shook.

In the morning a train went by, rattling everything in the house. Open windows banged shut by themselves. I sat on the edge of the bed, awakened by the noise. I'd been dreaming about Marianne's father, a boy I barely knew except for his mouth and the dull weight of his hips. In the dream I see the Chevelle parked in our yard, the white paint shimmering pink and blue in the sun. A ripe orange falls from a neighbor's tree onto the hood, plunk, and rolls to the street. He stands inside the door and, without words, I know what is expected of me. I do not undress, but I am back on the tiled floor again, the blue-gray slate under the dim hall light. My mother's green umbrella leans beside the door, my shoulder blades push against the ice-cold tile. Somewhere up the carpeted steps my mother sleeps, dreamless.

I crouched on the edge of the bed, far from Marianne, my knees pulled up close to my chest. The train and the dream seemed the same, and I tried to hold my breath until it passed, but the rumbling and clattering didn't stop so I gave up and breathed in the dust and grease sifting under the door. I tasted the memory in my mouth, sharp, unwanted. The train moaned in the distance, the iron bulk of it now past our house, the dust settling at the foot of the bed. And I was filled with guilt and shame for the thing, though I do not remember ever wanting to do it, and I do not remember ever saying I would. Suddenly I was sick, hunched retching over a brown plastic wastebasket. I watched Marianne turn and sigh, and sleep on.

This afternoon Jeffrey showed up at the front door, wearing the same green army coat with the brass buttons, but looking younger in the daylight with a blond beard that must have grown overnight. Marianne hid in the bedroom for two hours, until Jeffrey made her a wand out of the TV aerial and some aluminum foil.

"It's magical," he said. She watched him through the crack in the door. "C'mon Marianne."

She tiptoed across the linoleum floor and slipped between my knees. "I still don't like you," she told him as she grabbed the wand. On her fingers she wore rings with colored plastic stones attached to tarnished metal bands.

"Do you have bells on your toes?" Jeffrey asked.

Marianne showed him her bare feet—rings on each of her big toes. She wiggled them at him and smiled. "How do you like that?" she asked.

"I like that a lot," he said. "You have very pretty feet."

Within minutes Marianne is showing him her dress-up clothes, modeling a flowered kimono and my patent pumps, taking him outside to look at the yard. They walk up the white gravel bed, step onto the railroad track, and wave at me where I lean in the frame of the back door with my arms wrapped around my waist. Marianne moves her shoulders up and down and claps her hands. She does a little dance on the track. The phone rings but I decide not to answer it. I am immovable in the doorway, watching them smiling at me, watching Jeffrey take Marianne's hand and help her down the graveled slant. Then they move toward me, fast, running, like people in a home movie.

For dinner we eat tacos from the fast food place down the street.

"Time for bed," I tell Marianne, but she shrieks, pulling away from me and leaping onto Jeffrey's lap.

"We're going to wait for the train tonight, Roxanna," she says. She picks up a crayon and, holding it between two fingers, raises it to her mouth and exhales.

Jeffrey looks at me but I try to avoid his eyes, which are sad and soft like a saint's. We go outside and unfold two of those old lounge chairs. It's almost dark, surprisingly cool.

"This is like spring in Massachusetts," I say.

"This is magic weather," Marianne whispers, clutching the wand. We adjust the chairs until they lean almost all the way back, and we push them close together so there is no gap. Marianne fits beside me, under my arm. Jeffrey drapes his big green coat over us all. Underneath it he holds my hand.

"What are we waiting for?" I ask.

"The magic circus train," Marianne says. She turns toward Jeffrey and he smiles.

I do not want her liking this man, climbing up onto his lap, believing in him, but I've grown tired of holding back. The bare yard dissolves in the dark, yet overhead the stars are blinding. My toes peek out from under the heavy coat, alive, covered with skin instead of moss.

While we wait for the train, I imagine a man tied to the tracks. I make out the shape of him—lying prone on top of the glowing white gravel—but the face of the man changes. It is Marianne's father, it is James Copper, and then it is Jeffrey with his pale blue eyes pleading, with his only possessions crammed in a duffel bag by the door. He will mark me in some way, like the rest, leave the imprints of his arms and fingerprints like tattoos under my clothes. I do not care. Marianne's breathing moves her against me, slow gentle breaths that spill out mist into the green night. She too will learn the cycle of things, the irresistible wheel that draws us into its spokes. Even now, as we sit in these lawn chairs, the three of us together under the dark wide sky and the over-bright stars, our lives happen—all around, just then, forever.

mouth of friend and stranger

I saw him first. He was safe in his group of friends, his friends cushioning us from each other. I didn't know him. I had my copy of Lowell, just purchased from the used bookstore, and I sat alone. We were at the Cuban restaurant, outdoors at the plastic patio tables lit by tiki torchlight. The mambo band played. Or we were in the dim space on the swiveling stools of the bar next door. We were passing each other on the sidewalk by the beauty salon in the Mediterranean-style plaza—Cuts for Ten Dollars. Any of those ways. He wore a pinstriped shirt. His hair was mussed. At first, nothing seemed to pass between us. He was from Missouri. He was a law student. Or he wrote poetry at Yale. He was an auto mechanic. He sold famous knives.

In his eyes I saw the boys who played baseball with the girls on the wide lawns of the street of my childhood. Their hands all knuckles, stuffed in their gloves. That intense look, the boy thing underneath, always something to prove. Chestnuts fell onto the lawn in their spiny casings. The leaves floated down, one by one. The fathers' cars sat shiny and streamlined in each driveway. The mothers' station wagons sat beside them, two long cars taking up little space in the scheme of the long winding tarred drives. Lampposts with yellow light. He could have been one of those boys, grown up. In him, I saw the games of manhunt and freeze tag, the scuffle of bodies in the dark, my childhood handprints glowing on the skin of his forearm.

I followed him into the restaurant. The steamy, heavy smell of the place—picadillo and roast pork, chorizo and boliche. The painted tables thrown together with their chairs on the cement floor. We stood by the restrooms and waited. The air freshener, the smell of the soap in the dispenser, the urine and stale perfume, seeped out under the doors. He looked at my legs, at the outlines of them all the way up under my skirt. I watched him look. Then I waited for him in the little hallway outside the bathroom door. As he passed me I grabbed the cuff of his sleeve. I held his arm captive, and he let me. He turned around, not very surprised. I felt the weight of the sleeve of his shirt, read the expression on his face, his eyebrows up, his mouth half-smiling, not ready to give in to anything.

"Sit with me," I said.

He shrugged and grinned. He was singled out, chosen. I was someone he was happy to have done this. Everything, at that point, pleased him.

You learned about presenting yourself. *Here I am,* you would say, rounding the stair landing, facing your parents and their friends in the dining room. A dinner party, Mrs. Winslow lolling, drunk on sidecars, my father in the kitchen filling fresh glasses. The men wore ties, the women silk dresses. In the dimmed chandelier light the food dried on the bone china, the candles burned down to their wicks. Everyone turned, everyone poured their attention. My mother with her eyes bright, distracted, the other women tight-lipped, the men rubbing their chins. I passed through the room and felt my hair swing along my waist, the back of my neck tightening, aware. I cut a swath through their silence. I felt the silence fall about me, pressing close enough to kiss.

In church, you held the missal just so in your hands. You bent your head, smiled sweetly, devout. Around you the fathers in their suits stank like the morning's hangover. The mothers' hands were veined and thin, their mouths drooped, tired in their lipstick. You smelled the sheets on their skin through their clothes. You felt their heat and guilt, their shining relief at the end, when we filed out into the morning sunlight, into spring and all the dogwoods blooming. I kept my hands folded. My thoughts were always chaste. In confession, I made up sins to say, my voice quaking with the sin of saying them.

Outside, his group of friends never missed him. I watched them laughing in the growing dark, in the torchlight, through the plate-glass window. We sat at an empty table inside and talked. We brushed aside the waitress suggesting drinks. Even then, we had other ideas. I told him things he didn't really care to hear. Who I was, where I was from, what it was like there this time of year, still buried under winter. He took the book from me, still in its bag from the bookstore, and slid it out. He held it in the palms of his hands and read the cover, rubbed his thumbs along the spine, and riffled the pages. *Life Studies.* Something dropped out onto the table.

"What's this?" he said. He picked it up and looked at it, some printed verse on heavy paper, the cover of a card. He read part of it out loud. His voice was low and bemused.

Christ be with me, Christ within me, Christ behind me, Christ before me, Christ beside me, Christ to win me, Christ to comfort and restore me. . . . He shook his head.

He handed it to me. It was decorated with a figure in robes, with prancing lambs holding staffs. On the back was a note to someone, written in a slanted hand.

"It's St. Patrick's breastplate. A charm," I told him. "To protect him against the Druids."

His eyes were doubtful of me. I slid my chair close. I put my leg up on his. He propped his face on one hand, still with that quizzical look.

"I like the bridge jumpers," I said. "Berryman. Kees?" I told him Berryman's father shot himself here in this city, in 1926.

"Where, do you think?" he asked.

"Maybe down the street, behind that stucco apartment building."

He glanced over his shoulder, slowly, toward the patio and his circle of friends. His fingers found the hem of my skirt and slid up.

"I like good old Tennyson," he said. "The early Swinburne."

Under the table things happened.

"Would I not hurt thee perfectly?" he said.

I leaned over and placed my forehead at the base of his neck. I breathed in the smell of him under his shirt. His hand swam up, his fingers graceful swimmers. Behind us the waitresses whispered, girls with dark, curling hair and red fingernails. He took my arm and we pushed the chairs back, and looked around. Who knows what you look for when your knees tremble at the swishing fabric of your skirt? A place with a door, a corner to drape yourself against him. A place to be supine, prostrate, to feel Swinburne's *delicious things—pleasure, sorrow, sleep, sin,* to *wax amorous.*

The palm of his hand was hot, concentrating on my fingers.

Once, my childhood girlfriend and I took a bedspread out into the pasture. We knew what we were doing, walking out there. We had a plan. At the base of my spine was a small tingle. It was April. The trees in the old apple orchard blossomed white and pink. Below the little wizened trunks, beneath the gnarled branches, the damp ground looked snow-covered. We laid the bedspread out on the white ground. We pulled the ends in around ourselves and took off our clothes. We pretended to be the babysitter with her boyfriend on the couch, the glow of the television lighting up her stomach's bared skin, his hand creeping up, their mouths pressed together. We knew to move against each other, to make soft moans. Under the canopy of flowers, with the smell of the wet new grass, we did not know what our pretending meant, where our bodies took us, close enough to being lovers. A man and woman came by, two strangers. The man held a pair of clippers. The woman's arms were full of blossoms. They looked at us on the spread. We were covered up, but our shoulders were bare, our skin flushed, giving them ideas. They looked at us a long time, wondering, then moved on.

With boys, we stumbled onto places. Hamonassett Beach, under a woolen blanket. A cold day, almost wintry, with a haze. The sea roared up and back. There were pebbles in the sand, mussel shells, breathtakingly sharp and glinting, the revelation of an arm with a wristwatch against the tempting darkness of the blanket's depths. You never wanted to emerge, blinking, to place yourself. You were underwater, all legs, all needy mouths, craving sustenance.

There was the front seat of a '64 Mustang, the gearshift impossibly placed, the pine tree air freshener dangling from the radio dial, something playing, headlights off, the backdrop the assorted wrecks of the Mobil station's lot. Or the back seat of his mother's Chrysler Country Squire, the long, vinyl seat cushion, the hot summer afternoon through all the wide windows, the tall reservoir grass waving outside, brushing against the tires, a few blackbirds perched to watch. There were basements, old recliners with torn upholstery, the throaty start of the furnace revving up, the smell of laundry detergent, dryer lint floating like milkweed. Or rec room shag between your shoulder blades, the record snagged on "Gold Dust Woman," the backyard floodlights triggered again and again by prowling neighborhood dogs, upstairs, the boy you really wanted with someone else.

Later, there was a bed in an apartment, or a house. And still, you ended up on the couch, in your grandmother's wing chair, in the tub, in the shower, steamy and scalded, the hot water always running out, the steam peeling the wallpaper. You missed the places you would find before, so you found them again.

He took my hand and we slipped down the restroom hallway, and outside, through the door to the alley. Acacia hung over a fence from someone's yard. It was dusk. I had left my book and the card behind on the table. The note had said: *To Lise, Do not forget to remember me, Charles.*

I wanted time to gather him in, to distinguish his face, but he placed his mouth on mine, and it dreamed up, out of nowhere, a place all its own. I let myself fall in. I was languid. I was mercuric. A warm breeze, eddies of it, circled in. He pressed me up against the brick wall. There was the exhaust fan's whirring, his soft open hands' sliding, the general disdainful clank of dishes. The yellow acacia blooms tumbled over into the cobblestones, into my hair. One tucked itself along his collar. The dishwasher came out in his dirty apron for a smoke. My skirt was up. Our clothes were luminous in the dim light.

The breeze brought the smoke by, mixed it with the acacia, the fruit trees in the backyards, the smell of fried plantains. The dishwasher looked, then looked away.

There was never space, but always some clever way to wriggle up or on top or beneath. Bucket seats and bench seats, vinyl or leather and armrests and contours you could not fit. Sometimes, spread out on starched white motel sheets. Golf courses and reservoirs and parks after hours. My knees in pine needles, my back against roots of trees, lake docks, the deck of tossing boats. In heatless cabins, surrounded by snow. The agonizing interruptions: policemen shining their flashlights, roommates wandering in, parents slamming doors downstairs. Clothes half off, damp skin stark in the glare. The boy's guilty glance up, his apology, his regret, everything dwindling to a kind of starving.

In the alley, his mouth wandered down. He held my arms back against the brick. I tasted everything I could along his neck. The rest of it: *Christ beneath me, Christ above me, Christ in quiet, Christ in danger, Christ in hearts of all that love me, Christ in mouth of friend and stranger.* At first you thought, *isn't just this mouth enough?* The different mouths of boys. New Year's Eve, fifteen, drunk on Chianti, two bottles we had been instructed to bring from our mother's house to that of a friend. We crossed the pasture in the snow, passing the heavy bottles, the snow crunching under our feet. Overhead the stars were out, blurry in the black night. The wine made our lips sweet. We went instead to a party. Inside the house was hot. I lost my coat. At midnight I started kissing boys, one after the other. Their mouths tasted different but the same. Their tongues slid around, quick or slow. I held each one to me, my hands on the backs of their necks, on their shoulders. I was passed on, like the bottle of wine. In the end, I found myself standing alone in the snow on the front lawn. One boy I'd kissed fought with his girlfriend, and put his fist through the garage door window, and the police came.

Later, you discovered the limitations of your mouth on his. It would go on. He would wear some sad, tortured guise. We would be breathless, getting nowhere, our lips numb, everything raw and overdone, the waiting drawn out like a tight wire. You wanted the end of it, even though you knew once it was over, you would not have a need to remember what you did not know of him to begin with. Your heart, free of grief and dreams, would be ready to move on.

His hands were soft and boyish. His hands were calloused and covered with brown hair. His fingers were thick and stubby. His hands, his fingers, were small and beautiful. I felt his face. I felt through his shirt—the collarbones, the tops of his arms, and underneath the planes of his chest. My hands dipped past his waist to the bones of his hips, below the undone button of his pants. My hands forgot themselves. It was always this: you give something and take something, until the edges blur and you are not sure if you are giving or taking enough, taking or giving too much. Then suddenly, clearly, you see that doesn't matter.

It was a selfish relinquishing. You wanted the ache of his mouth, to be ravished. Some of them refused to do it. They were afraid of themselves, of everything waiting, feverish, under my clothes. I let them pretend to love me, to profess it, like a password, like a secret code. His voice was soft and lulling. His voice was hoarse with longing. He told me what he wanted. He told me nothing, and guided my hands. In the shadows thrown by cars' map lights, in the deep ends of pools, our legs thrashing strangely pale, on the countertops of kitchens, there was the silent language of need, the repository of wordless inquiries and assents. He grabbed my hair and pulled me down, he put his hands on my shoulders and gave a little push.

The way it should have been: I learn his name. He invites me to sit with his friends, finds another plastic chair and pulls it in. We listen to the mambo band. We fan away mosquitoes. Sitting together, I find little to say, and never talk about the poets who took their lives. I bum a cigarette and sit silently, seeming mysterious. Maybe the boy across the table, the one I never noticed, likes me better. He will be the one, later, to ask me out. I will think, wistfully, longingly, of someone else. There will be a time set, a place to meet. He will decide, *well, what of her?* I will never love him. This in the alley would never have happened with him.

This: the weeds between the cobblestones, the litter of wilted petals, the remains of the dishwasher's smoke, me pressed against the brick. The back of his shirt wet. I heard my own breathing, ragged and soft, his voice, still bemused, saying things into my hair. His hands held my face, slid down and up again, finding me with his palms, his thumbs. I was mute, catching my breath. His eyes closed. I watched him keep them that way, until the end. It was done when his hands dropped away like stones. I clung to him and he zipped his pants. He placed his mouth on my neck. He brushed my hair from my face, and stepped back, adjusting his clothes. He left with the delicate, telling part of him I could never urge with my tongue. I heard his footfalls. Through the kitchen's screen door I heard the dishwasher clear his throat.

I was *the girl who does know better but.* I was the newspaper, folded and abandoned on the train. I was the whore tidying her room, achy and pleased. I was the woman driving home with the secret between my legs. I was poised on the rail of the bridge, clutching the cables, caught by the wind, euphoric with the desire to douse myself in cold, black water. Berryman waved to the people first. "Here I go," he must have said, stepping off into his high-flung moment.

He went back to his friends at the table. In the torchlight and the din of too much beer, no one detected my traces. Once in a while, I looked for him. But he had left for Cambridge, he was running drugs from Haiti, working the Alaskan pipeline, teaching English in Japan. He was never there to refute me and so he surrendered himself to my memory.

Some nights, I dreamed he told me everything.

Later. At last. I said I knew him.

the returning

The night Fay's grandmother died a balmy wind shook the leaves on the mango trees in the backyard. Everyone gathered at the house, which the Realtor, later, advertised for sale as a "dollhouse." It was Fay and her father and her aunt and uncle. Fay's mother stayed at home. "Call me when it's over," she told Fay from her bedroom. Fay could not remember what her mother had been doing, just that she had called to her on the stairs, and the door had been open only a crack, and the darkness beyond the lit stairwell seemed dense and unfathomable. Fay was twelve. The mango leaves in the wind had reminded her of pompoms. Her grandmother had been moved from the hospital, where she would not die, into her own bedroom at home, and Fay and her aunt laid down on either side of her on the double bed, and Fay's father and uncle went outside for a cigarette. It was Fay who noticed a settling calm about the covers, and woke her aunt. They went out into the backyard, and Fay's uncle pointed out the full moon, and Fay's father took the cigarette from his mouth and sang out part of a popular song on the radio at the time, one that opened with a tribal chant, "Hey yeh yah!"

Years later, when Fay gave birth to her daughter, she would look at the shape of her baby's bald skull and recall, fleetingly, her grandmother with her wig off, dying under the layer of pale green comforter. Fay and her neighbor both had babies at the same time and they would push them in strollers around their neighborhood and wonder if their husbands were having affairs. Her neighbor, Vionet, was ten years older, wore dark lipstick and sunglasses, and radiated a sultry distance that intimidated Fay, who despite her advantage of youth, her hair its own natural color, her body still slim and boyish, could not walk beside Vionet without feeling plain and despairing.

"Why do you think he would sleep with someone else?" Fay asked her. It was an early morning walk, and Vionet had her coffee mug. Her baby, Claude, was asleep under a blue checked blanket.

"Because," she began. She gulped her coffee. Her hand on the stroller handle was white at the knuckles. Fay heard the sand and pebbles grind under the rubber tires. She listened to the garbage truck accelerate on the next street. Her own baby, Sylvie, made a squeaking sound, and Fay reached around and replaced the pacifier in her mouth.

"I don't think he can get back to that moment anymore," Vionet said.

It was October, approaching the date that Fay's grandmother died. The air, nudged into currents, dislodged petals from the flowering trees. The light on the lawn changed its slant through the wood blinds. It was this way every year.

"What do you mean?" she asked Vionet. She looked over at her, but could not determine anything beneath the calm, slightly flushed cheek, the hair tightly pulled back, the black sunglasses reflecting nothing.

"You know," Vionet said. "It's how you stay in love. You can place yourself back into the moment you first felt something for him. You return."

Fay nodded. "Oh, yes." Fay often pretended to understand things she did not. It was safer than voicing an objection. But she could not remember a single moment when she knew she loved her husband. To which moment out of the manifold moments, she wondered, should she return? Their days were full of small kindnesses that Fay had always accepted as love. She ironed his shirts. He placed diagonals of toast on a plate with her tea. She was still moved by some unspoken tenderness when he came home after a haircut, and she saw the pale place above his ears revealed. To which moment would he return? she wondered now. It was not the sort of thing she would ever ask.

"So," Fay said, "He's forgotten."

Vionet stopped in the street so abruptly that Fay ended up several paces ahead.

"Maybe," Vionet said. Her coffee had sloshed out onto her hand, and she wiped it on the jacket she had tied around her waist.

"Remind him," Fay suggested. "Make a new one."

Vionet began walking again. "He may have made a *new one* with someone else," she said. Fay could only read the shape of Vionet's mouth, a down-turned line, the wry emphasis she placed on the words.

"If yours was first, it may take precedence."

Vionet stopped again. She lowered her sunglasses and stared at Fay.

"Of course mine wasn't *first,*" she said. She confided in Fay that her husband had been married when he met Vionet, that they had been sleeping together when the wife found out and filed for divorce. Fay wanted to know how the wife had found out, if they had been caught in bed together, or she had discovered a charge receipt for a motel, or simply a long, dark hair on his shirt. They had walked the strollers into the local park, and placed them in the shade. The park was empty this early. Vionet lit a cigarette.

"No," she said. She blew smoke rings, like Fay and her friends did in high school, and looked over at Fay and grinned. "Don't you want one?" She held the cigarette out to Fay, its filter reddened by her lipstick. When Fay smoked she was beset with longing for some other life, and so she rationed herself to one a day. Soon, the babies would wake up, and she would go home and start her routine. Later, if the babies slept at the same time, Fay might go over and lie out in the sun on Vionet's terracotta patio in her swimsuit, and Vionet might make them sloe gin fizzes, or margaritas, or some other drink from the recipe book kept by the blender on her kitchen counter, and then Fay would have her cigarette. And if not then, then much later, at night outside in her own walled courtyard shrouded by crepe myrtle and bamboo, where against the backdrop of the sky a cloud formed like magician's smoke.

On the metal bench, Vionet sighed. "He told her," she said. "He felt he *owed* it to her." A group of preschoolers was let out of the building behind them. Their little shrieks woke Claude, then Sylvie. Fay wanted to take Vionet's hand and squeeze it, to reassure her. She could not imagine waiting for such an inevitable moment—a husband arriving home from work, blank-faced, pitiable in his need to unburden himself of his guilt.

Fay knew about infidelity from her grandmother. Fay's grandfather had divorced her grandmother for someone else late in life, and she had ended up in her little cottage by the Air Force base with her dog, Ollie, and her cats, Ricket and Sundry, and her bottle of vodka hidden in the litterbox. She had squandered her divorce settlement money on elaborate Christmas gifts for her children and for Fay—TVs and dolls with expensive accessories, bicycles and sets of blue, leather-bound Encyclopedia Britannica for each household. When they refused the gifts she cried and drank and pulled what Fay's father called "a lockout," and so they all saw it made her happy, spending her money, and for the next few years they let her. Fay determined now that her grandmother's divorce had triggered this miserable outcome, first poverty, then alcoholism, then cancer. She only half-believed that her ownership of the entire American Girl doll collection, stored away in boxes for Sylvie, had anything to do with it.

Fay and Vionet walked home. Claude screamed from his stroller, his little face red and scrunched. Sylvie was plugged with her pacifier and sucked vigorously. Watching her, Fay felt her breasts tighten. Vionet moved quickly, spurred by Claude's wails. The sun warmed up the pavement. The bougainvillea draped in places over the sidewalk. Fay thought of nothing but feeding Sylvie, settling into the cushion of the couch, closing her eyes and smelling Sylvie's hair and her own milk. Neither of them paid any attention to the car. It came from behind, a heavy sedan with a sun-faded hood. Its driver, the tiny news article would claim, was an elderly woman named Mrs. Henry Culligan who lived with her sister and hadn't driven in years. The car approached the intersection and sat there idling for an unusual length of time. Fay remembered its taillights blinking on and off, on and off. She smelled its exhaust. And then Vionet crossed the street. Did she look back to check on Fay? Fay worried over this later. Mrs. Culligan began to turn and then, the reports claimed, seeing she should not, grew flustered and pressed her foot to the gas instead of the brake. The car's impact was unavoidable. It could not be taken back, nor could its striking the stroller, and sparing Vionet. Fay watched Vionet make a flaying movement with her arms, her fingers grasping air. Her sunglasses fell to the sidewalk. Fay remembered her own mouth opening and no scream coming out. Just her heart stopped in her chest, a dull, impenetrable silence. Around them the silence expanded, wide and encompassing. Fay felt that she and Vionet had been caught there like insects under a large glass.

Much later, Fay would remember other details. Vionet's bloody clothes and hands, Fay's own T-shirt soaked with milk. How when the paramedics arrived they had to lift them both up from the pavement where they sat, clutching their babies. Fay would not look when they tried to take Claude from Vionet's arms. Her own child cried, full and piercing. The paramedic asked her if Sylvie was all right.

"She's hungry," Fay said, dumbly, her legs weak.

The man looked down at her shirt, and flushed. "OK," he said, backing off. He was young, with a freshly shaven chin, and small, competent hands that held Fay's elbows in a way that made her think of a lover.

Vionet and Fay did not talk much after. Vionet kept to herself. She and her husband moved to another neighborhood, and Fay heard that she had another baby, which is what Fay would have suggested she do, if Vionet had ever asked. In the new neighborhood, among different people, Vionet could walk the baby, and no one would think about Claude. No one would even know, unless Vionet chose to tell them. Though she missed Vionet, had loved her like a sister, Fay understood that things were never forgotten, deaths and births and the moments of recognizing love. You simply stepped away from them and kept silent, and the idea of forgetting them occurred to you, as close and sweet as a kiss.

Fay took Sylvie with her to her mother's on the weekends with a packed bag so Fay and her husband could go out. Lately, though, Fay had been going out with her girlfriends, and her husband stayed home, happy enough to eat leftovers, or grab take-out and watch television. He thought Fay and her friends went to movies and out for coffee afterwards. Instead, Fay went to downtown clubs housed in old three-story brick buildings, with expensive sound systems and crowds of men and women brushing hips and shoulders, spilling drinks on each other's shoes. Fay would choose a man to smile at, or bum a cigarette from. He would lean his face into her hair to say things to her, and maybe, she might lead him into a dark corner to let him kiss her. She would go home with her friends and slip into her own bed beside her husband, her body tight and singing with the memory of someone else.

Tonight, Fay dropped off Sylvie early, at five o'clock. Sylvie was two and clung to her and did not want her to go. Her face contorted, and Fay felt a pang of alarm.

"Nana wants you to play," Fay said.

Fay's mother had on her floor-length caftan. She clapped her hands at Sylvie and sang part of a Halloween song. "Stir it in my witches brew, I've got magic, Alacazamacazoo!" Fay's mother owned a nursery school, which Sylvie attended part-time during the week. Spread out on the surface of the satin bedcover were orange pumpkin cut-outs and black triangles the children would paste on for eyes and a nose. Fay's mother reached out and put a hand on Sylvie's arm. Her hair had been done that day, styled up stiff with spray. She wore her half-glasses on a chain. In the bedroom was the old, familiar smell of clean bed sheets and cigarettes and the unique mix of Beefeaters and White Shoulders. Did Fay notice her mother's swaying a bit more than usual? She hesitated and allowed Sylvie to cling to her.

"Maybe I'll just take her home," Fay said.

Her mother gave her a look. "What are you talking about?" she said. "I've made her dinner." She put her hands on her hips. Fay did hear a slur in her speech.

A scene was coming. Fay could leave as quickly as possible with Sylvie, but that would not be the end of it. Her mother was used to

Sylvie spending every weekend with her. She had come to depend on it, and Fay saw that she would not let her forget. The calls would start as soon as she got home. She would threaten to tell Fay's husband where Fay really went. She would hang up and call back, over and over with new threats and accusations. She would curse Fay and say that she had always chosen her grandmother over her. Fay never realized, before her mother's drunken calls, that her mother had expected her to stay with her on the night of her grandmother's death, that all along a rivalry had been going on for rights to Fay's love.

The October light fell across the carpet and wavered there. Beyond the glass doors was the cement patio covered with an aluminum awning, the square of backyard grass, and the swing where Fay's mother would rock Sylvie to sleep as an infant. This house was not the one where Fay grew up. It was a smaller, cement-block place that her mother bought when she divorced Fay's father. Her mother slammed her hand down on the bedside table. "Why would you do this?" she said. Her face was red, her voice shrill. Sylvie began to cry. Fay breathed in slowly. She had planned to meet her friends early, at six, for dinner, and she was tempted to just go, to leave Sylvie and let her mother pacify her. Hadn't she left her every other weekend with only slight reservations? She wanted her mother to be happy. Fay sighed, and gave Sylvie a little push in her mother's direction. She went out the front door and stood on the front walk, waiting for the crying to stop. Her chest tightened. She felt her heart beat at the base of her throat. Sylvie's crying continued, anguished and unceasing. Fay imagined her daughter's mottled face, her little hands in fists, rubbing her eyes.

When Fay was small her grandmother would watch her in the afternoons after school. She would pick her up in her car filled with cigarette smoke. She would have her drink glass in the cup holder and her cigarettes in a lamé case. She had her hair done twice a week, and the style was full and formal, like a girl's on prom night. She always wore her rings and her makeup, applied in a specially lighted mirror in her bedroom. Her grandmother drove erratically, with fierce turns that slid Fay into the passenger door. Fay would realize that her grandmother's drinking impaired her driving ability when she drove drunk herself and experienced the same buoyant fearlessness. As a child, Fay did not know to be afraid. Fay's grandmother would say, "Ooops!" and "Whoa!" and Fay would laugh and grab onto the back of the seat. They would get to her house, the one she lived in with her grandfather, the Bermuda ranch with the plantation shutters and the freshly cut lawn, and Fay's grandmother would make them both a snack, which they would eat out by the pool. Faye's grandmother called it "the lagoon." Sometimes, her grandmother would fall asleep on the chaise, and Fay would sit with her pile of books and puzzles or her dolls and play quietly, waiting for her grandmother to wake up. Once, her grandmother slept until it grew dark, and the landscape lights came on and shivered on the pool's surface. Fay had reached out and touched her grandmother's bare foot and given it a little shake. The foot had been slightly swollen and threaded with thin veins. Her grandmother sat up, suddenly, and looked around blinking like one of Fay's dolls. It was chilly. Fay's grandfather came out from the house in his suit, his shoe soles tapping on the patio tiles. "What are my two girls doing out here?" He grinned. Fay's grandmother looked up at him in dismay, and later Fay would wonder if her grandmother knew that his geniality came from having just left his girlfriend's bed.

Fay listened to Sylvie cry. She did not know how to be a mother, she thought. She went back into the house. Sylvie sat in her little time-out chair in the corner of Fay's mother's bedroom.

"What are you doing, Fay?" her mother said. She came out of the bathroom with her glass. Fay knew then that her mother kept her liquor bottle there, hidden in a cupboard. She had looked for it many times while her mother was busy with Sylvie, searching behind bags of potting soil on dim garage shelves, beneath the stacked placemats in the dining room buffet.

"I don't feel like going out," Fay said.

Fay's mother glared at her. "You will teach her that she can get away with anything," she said.

Fay looked over at Sylvie. She sat quietly now, watching, her chest heaving with little sighs. She did not dare leave the time-out chair. She was a good girl, and the bow in her hair tonight was grosgrain, patterned with ladybugs, and Fay loved her. She held her arms out to her, and Sylvie ran into them gratefully. Her dress, which Fay had pressed that morning, smelled of spray sizing. Her skin was damp from the exertion of crying. Fay hefted her daughter up into her arms and left the room. Behind her, she knew her mother had probably begun to cry. While she put Sylvie into the car her mother stood at the front door and called to her.

"Don't do this, Fay," she called. "Please."

Fay ignored her. A neighbor who passed with his dog looked away. Fay's mother kept on from the doorway, her voice plaintive and awful. Fay got quickly into the car and drove home. She would unplug the phone from the wall. Or, better, she would convince her husband to take them somewhere—a nice hotel at the beach, a family vacation. As she drove she made these plans, deciding what to pack, her heart soft and fluttering in her chest. Sylvie fell asleep in her car seat, her legs with their chubby knees lax and dangling. Fay hated to see her sleep in her clothes. She wanted to take off her shoes and the little ruffled socks. She wanted to lie down and pull her daughter's body close to hers.

At her house, Fay fumbled with the keys to the door. Inside, the lights were off, and Fay was surprised to see her husband was not there in front of the television. She wondered now how she might convince him of her plans when she did not know where he'd gone and she was annoyed. She carried Sylvie, still asleep, upstairs to the master bedroom. She would not tell him what really happened. She would lie, and say that her mother was sick. She planned to put Sylvie down on her bed, and then retrieve her nightgown from her own room, but in the hallway to the bedroom Fay stopped. She sensed a slight disruption in the dimness, a sound of movement and breath. She heard two people, a man and a woman on the bed. Their sighs grew, and Fay listened to her own husband's moans with a sudden, wrenching embarrassment. She stood in the hallway shadows. She felt Sylvie's weight. Her arms began to ache. Yet, even when they were through, and the woman slid from the bed and came to the doorway, Fay could not move. The woman paused there on the threshold, nude, stunned to stillness. Faye saw the white shine of her skin, her luminous thighs and breasts, a slender arm upraised, holding a glass. Fay did not look at her face, into her eyes. The woman made a small noise, one of protest and surprise. Fay turned away quickly and retreated down the stairs. Outside, she hurried to the car and put Sylvie in and slid behind the wheel. She did not know where she would go.

The night her grandmother died Fay and her aunt watched the ambulance attendants bring her home and lay her down on her bed. It was very late. In the hospital, there had been no need for her wig. She wore a nightgown that Fay's aunt had picked out, cotton, trellised with roses. They pulled up the covers, and the hospice worker, who would depart until morning, told them all would be fine now, that this was what Fay's grandmother wanted. Fay remembered that she had been in awe of her grandmother's will not to die until she got her way. Her father and her uncle had been annoyed, inconvenienced. Fay's aunt had been up for two days, waiting and crying.

"I need to sleep," her aunt said.

Her aunt lay down alongside Fay's grandmother, and Fay stretched out, too, on the other side. The air in the little house was close. It smelled of dirt and leaves traipsed in on the bottoms of their shoes and milk spoiled in saucers in the next room. Sitting behind the wheel of her car, Fay remembered that the night her grandmother died she had been thinking about her routine for cheerleading, the boy in homeroom who wrote his name on the palm of her hand. His eyes had been brown and thickly lashed. He held her hand in his and pressed lightly with the tip of the pen. Her grandmother gasped, agonizing breaths with long stretches of silent space between them. Fay and her aunt each took one of her grandmother's hands. Fay thought, *give up give up give up.* Around them the little house was still and fragile. The window curtains came in and out like her grandmother's breathing. Fay felt the air, and heard the leaves on the mango trees, imagined the sound like shimmering.

Fay could suddenly see the moments to which she would always return. They revealed themselves, a tableau of selfish horrors. She remembered baby Claude's accident, not the way it happened, but the way she imagined it might have, with herself and Sylvie in the path of Mrs. Culligan's car. It could easily have been them. Sylvie would be the baby thrown from the stroller. There was her little pacifier in the grass by the curb. And then Fay skipped ahead, through the grief of that moment and on into the years beyond, when the grief would have dulled and dimmed to something precious, like a talisman. She would not have had any more children. She and her husband would have separated, not from sorrow, but from a lack of any reason to remain together. She would enter into the future alone—years unfolding shining and strange, full of people she would never meet, lovers and friends, places she would never live.

She saw her grandmother's head, round and bare on the pillow, her mouth open like a baby bird's. Her body was a husk, ready to be abandoned, but Fay knew now that as she had lain beside her planning her own life out beyond the inexorable, lengthening breathing, her grandmother never wanted to go. Fay rolled down the car window. She smelled the vine flowering in her courtyard. The lights in her house came on. She would wait for her husband to emerge and confess. She imagined his face, the sorrowful eyes, his pale lips mouthing a plea for forgiveness, like a moment she had been expecting all her life.

dead boyfriends

In the lot behind Junior's garage, buried in tall summer grass, are the hulls of cars in which Nan once had sex. Above her the elms wave and whine with insects. She treads the grass down in her sandals. Her hair sticks to her forehead, the back of her neck. Junior saunters along ahead of her with his same slanting shoulders and slouch, his black stringy hair threaded with gray now. They aren't looking for anything in particular yet. She had gone to the garage and knocked on the scarred wooden door in back, and he had opened it and stood there, nodding at her, his large dark eyes blank.

"You don't really remember me, do you?" she asks him now.

He stops and looks back over his shoulder. He holds a cigarette in his blackened fingers, and points. "That," he says. "That was Matt Olander's classic Buick."

Nan feels a little saddened lurch. The car seems hunched over in the grass. Nan sees that the front end is crushed, shoved in up to the dashboard. The paint still holds its glimmer of metal flake. Queen Anne's lace grows up around the back bumper.

"What happened to it?" she asks.

Junior says nothing for a long moment. He has always been quiet. He brings his cigarette to his mouth and takes a drag. His hair still falls over his eyes, Nan notices, so you can't read his face. "Run into a tree," he says.

Not Matt, she thinks. Matt Olander worked on cars in the Mobil station's bay. Later, they surmised it was the asbestos in the brakes that gave him the lung cancer that killed him. She used to ride with him in the '56 Buick convertible to the Berlin Turnpike motel. The red vinyl seats smelled of years of men's hair pomade. Matt's hands smelled of the soap he used to take off the grease. Nan doesn't feel anything about his death. It happened years after she knew him, when he had married and even had children. These things, even more than his death, surprise her. As if once she left him, he should have persisted in the same manner, like Junior, found easily this afternoon in the same place she last saw him.

She had come home to visit her old high school friend, Betty Barnard who, like Nan, had recently divorced. Betty had moved back into her mother's house, a place Nan spent a lot of time in as a teenager. On an impulse, without calling first, Nan packed a bag for herself and one for Clemmy, while he watched, quiet and wide-eyed from the center of the unmade king-sized bed. She told him, as she packed, all about her friend Betty from school, making her seem like one of his own friends from preschool class, friends he missed with a perceptible sorrow since the initiation of summer. She realized the words tumbled from her mouth, that her movements had become frantic, but too late. As she closed the flap of the small suitcase, Clemmy flinched.

"Oh, stop it," she said, riddled with guilt. She held out her arms and he climbed into them. He smelled of buttered breakfast toast. The traffic was thick from Boston, and the drive to Connecticut took nearly three hours. Clemmy sat, as he always did, a perfect child in his car seat, his little books spread out within reach. After only an hour of driving, he fell asleep. Nan had heard horrors from other mothers of children throwing things, or shrieking, or twisting out from under their straps, and she had not understood any of it. She drove into town and went to Betty's mother's house, a split-level ranch in a subdivision off Terry Plains Road. The neighborhood seemed shadowy and deteriorated, the trashcans rolling on the sidewalks, the lawns full of crabgrass. She realized then that the trees had grown. The maples and elms, once new saplings braced with wires, were lofty, canopying the street. Nan remembered the times she ran away and went to see Betty, whose divorced mother smoked long Benson & Hedges menthols and went out ballroom dancing. Nan would hear her keys fumbling in the lock at night, her giddy laughter. She would kick off her pumps, one at a time, into the closet of the next bedroom. Sometimes she would come into Betty's room and flip on the light and look at them on the twin beds. She'd pause there, as if she wanted to say something but thought better of it, her earrings dangling a kind of music. Nan feigned sleep, feeling the bright overhead light against her lids, wondering when she might be loved enough. Betty had a rec room and a stereo, and Betty and Nan began having boys over, Betty upstairs in her own bedroom, and Nan downstairs on the rec room couch. Nan's father would eventually search her out, pulling into the driveway on a day she had not shown up at school. He would come to the door, his gaunt face mask-like. Nan remembered hiding up in Betty's pink painted room, peering at him from the upstairs window.

"I know you're up there," he would say, stepping back and looking up at the window.

Nan would feel a certain sadness, staring at his shoes planted on the cement porch. They were his dress shoes, the ones he buffed with a soft cloth on Sundays before church. She would think of her own room at home, its dormer window looking out over the apple orchard in spring, the blossoms white and pink on the uneven ground, the smell of her mother's clothes left hanging in her parents' bedroom closet. Yet she would not relent. She watched him and let him leave, the part of her that had torn healed over in the boys' clumsy arms, a hastily seamed scar.

This afternoon, when she arrived back in town, neither Betty nor her mother was home. Nan sat in her car in their driveway and did not know what to do. Clemmy still slept, his little hands in fists on his lap. She left a note on the screen door and considered driving to a motel rather than facing her father just yet. Nan did not often come home to visit. She was the youngest, the one everyone considered the most selfish. Her two sisters lived within proximity and cooked and cleaned and cared for their father as if he were infirm. Nan had moved far enough away, first to college in Rhode Island, then to Boston, so that she did not have to participate in any of the daily tending. Her father, when she saw him on holidays, always seemed perfectly capable and robust. She sat in Betty's mother's driveway a while longer. It was noon, and neither she nor Clemmy had eaten since early that morning. The air was still and heavy with humidity. She smelled the stink of the trashcans mixed with the scent of cut grass and gasoline. And then she had the feeling that Betty was up in her old pink bedroom, peeking out at her, waiting for her to leave. It was an odd feeling of reversal. Nan saw herself as the one with nothing to offer.

She decided to drive to her father's. He lived in the house she grew up in, an older farmhouse set back from the narrow road, with a screened-in front porch and two gables and beds full of flowers—daisy and black-eyed Susan, delphinium and larkspur. Around the side of the house grew hydrangea, heavy with blooms. The country club had purchased the back pastures years ago and tamed and groomed the wild grass into golf course greens. The barn had burned the year after Nan's mother died. It was a relic of the days when the farm was operating, a high, empty space filled with molding hay, and the fire was cited as accidental, unknown teenagers playing with matches. But after the fire her father gave up hope. It happened quickly, a kind of deflating. His face sagged around his cheeks. His eyes dulled. Most people said it had to do with the inexplicable nature of events, one after the other, but Nan always believed her father thought she had burned down the barn. Her tires crunched the gravel drive, past the orchard, the trees gnarled and old. Her father came right away at her knock and let her in, propping the screen door with a look of genuine surprise.

"You're here," he said.

He held her in a stiff embrace. His shirtfront smelled the same, like loam and soap flakes.

"Where's the boy?" he asked, stepping back. She saw his face brighten.

"Asleep still, in the car," she said.

Her father bounded down the steps and across the yard. Nan watched him extricate Clemmy from his car seat and carry him, still groggy, up onto the porch. Her father set him on his feet in the kitchen, and Nan saw that Clemmy had wet his pants. The front of her father's shirt was dampened from carrying him. "A little accident, I see," her father said. He knelt by Clemmy, grinning, his sharp chin jutting out.

"We're still working on that," Nan said. Her son's hair was rumpled from the long drive. He was small for his age, but sturdy and smart. He had been potty-trained at two and a half, and this was new, one of a number of reversions that she witnessed with a sinking sense of irreversibility, as if they would accumulate until he had returned to his infancy, a time she found herself the most incompetent. Nan opened Clemmy's bag and pulled out some dry clothes to change him, and then her father offered to do it, and Nan gratefully sank down into her old spot at the pine table in the kitchen. She could hear her father and Clemmy in the bathroom, her father's boisterous encouragements, and Clemmy's soft and higher-pitched replies. After, Clemmy colored at the table, and her father stood at the counter and made him a sandwich. He set out the old plaid beanbag ashtray, and she told him she had quit. "I'm impressed," he said. His face beamed. Perhaps he was, she thought. This was all it took. She assumed he would not mention her husband, who had met another woman and asked for the divorce, but then he did, anyway.

"Richard stopped in last week," he said.

Nan said nothing, and her father turned back to the counter.

"Well, he was in town," he said, carefully.

"What for?" Nan asked, her voice a little shrill.

Her father put his hand on the refrigerator handle.

"We went fishing," he said. "Like we always do."

The air in the kitchen was heavy, laden with the smell of that morning's cooked bacon. The windows were open, and her mother's lace curtains puffed out into the room and then pulled back against the old screens. The sills were filled with the dry wings of bees. Flies landed on the tabletop and the old aqua Formica counter. There was the cracked porcelain sugar bowl with its glued lid. On one end of the long table where her father's chair was pushed back, a game of solitaire spread like a map of his loneliness. He offered her a sandwich or something to drink, but she refused. He stood there, unable to find anything to do or say.

"Will you stay the night?" he asked her. Clemmy pulled apart his sandwich and poked at the peanut butter with his finger. Nan said she might, that she would take their things upstairs, and she rose from the table and went up to her old room. She sat on the edge of the bed and tried to remember someone she might call, but she could not. She stared at her little bookshelf lined with *Nancy Drews*, all in numerical order, their yellow spines faded. The room was still decorated the way her mother had planned it, with porcelain cats and white painted furniture, a room for a twelve-year-old girl. From the window she saw her father outside with Clemmy, busying himself in the flowerbeds. He had given the boy a watering can and she watched him fill it from the hose. Nan unpacked Clemmy's things. She pulled open the bureau drawers and placed the folded clothes inside, on top of the curling shelf paper. Her sisters would be around soon enough to discover her. There would be Rose's calm gaze and her crossed arms, May's endless questions. They would arrive with their own children, suntanned and noisy and barefoot, to swim in the pool her father had put in out back—an above-ground structure that resembled a barrel.

Nan went out onto the porch and asked her father if he would watch Clemmy while she drove into town for something at the store.

"What do you need?" he asked her. He stood among the phlox. She found him changed—his eyes searching, difficult to face. "I might have it."

Nan shrugged. "I feel like a drive," she said.

His shoulders fell, resigned. He nodded. She watched him take Clemmy by the hand and wave as she backed out of the driveway. Clemmy's small hand flipped brightly in imitation of his grandfather.

She drove down Tunxis Avenue with no place to go. The row of shaggy hickories shadowing the road parted, and Junior's was there, the first garage before Filley Pond and the center of town. She remembered when she and Matt Olander would stop in to visit Junior, usually on a Saturday night before they went out. Matt would have beer in a cooler, and she would follow him through the wooden door with its jangling bell, into the garage's sticky heat. Junior and Matt would chain-smoke and drink. Nan would sit, ignored, on a swivel chair with a ripped vinyl cushion. She'd worn pale-colored summer clothes and worried about getting grease on them. Her mother had been dead for nearly two years. She was in high school, and Matt was the first boy she slept with.

Now, Junior stands amid the cicada noise in the late summer haze. Nan drops down onto the front seat of a car that is only a rusted frame. She tucks her silk skirt under her legs. The upholstery is sun-faded and its stuffing comes out in tufts. She imagines the seat is a bed for mice. She is light-headed, her limbs loose. Earlier, inside the garage, he offered her a beer, and she took it, and then another, and perhaps another after that. She doesn't remember. She found the same torn vinyl swivel chair and that prompted her to talk about the past, recounting the stories she overheard Matt and Junior tell twenty years before, when all of their friends could be identified by the cars they worshipped and drove in rings around town or raced between the tobacco tents on Dudley Town Road. She did not tell him how she knew the stories or who she was. Junior didn't ask. He leaned up against an old Chevy truck and listened, every so often tossing his hair back or smiling, but saying nothing. Somehow, she revealed to him that she'd had sex in most of her boyfriend's cars, and he tipped his chin up at that and laughed out loud. He said he saw to it that most of his friend's cars ended up in his back lot, and that took them out the wooden door with its tinkling bell, around the side of the garage on a dirt path under the elms.

Junior pulls a beer from the back pocket of his baggy jeans. He takes a long sip and brings it over to Nan. She crosses her legs and kicks her sandaled foot. Her feet are dusty, she notices. She takes the beer, still cool from the garage refrigerator, and drinks.

"Most of them are dead," she says now. She says it lightly, carelessly.

Junior doesn't ask for the beer back. He lights another cigarette and watches her drink, his dark eyes like black pools. "Which ones?" he asks.

Nan remembers that Junior's reticence is not from shyness. It is purposeful, premeditated. In her memory he is back against a wall or leaning up against a car or a doorframe. There are groups of boys and girls, all paired up, teasing and playful, the boys' hands free, the girls leaning in with their mouths. Junior never had a girlfriend, she recalls. He watched them all from under his hair and made his occasional dry comments. A lean, lonely man, wreathed in his silence. She thinks for a moment.

"Stevie Ash," she says. "With the chainsaw scar from here to here." She points with her index finger from her neck, down across her chest.

Junior nods and exhales. "His family cut trees for firewood."

Nan remembers Stevie telling her the story, how the chain broke and flew up, a slick, clean swipe he didn't feel at first. It was a fall day, he said, and the wet leaves on the ground were splattered with what he realized was his own blood. The chain missed the carotid artery and he lived, but only a handful of years before his car rolled and rolled, broke the guardrail, and fell from the Tariffville Bridge.

"A Barracuda," she says. Silvery blue, like the real fish.

Junior motions for her to follow him, and he finds the car in the shade near the back of the lot, most of its paint seared off. Moths flutter up and around the lower tree branches.

"We would drive up to Highland Lake and park," she says. She remembers the brownish mud shore and the shine of the water on the dashboard. She'd slid her mouth along his scar, down to his waist. "Don't you want to see how far it goes?" he'd asked. Her pearl-colored fingernails played with the clasp to his pants. Sometimes families drove by and saw, but he would have his hands in her hair and say it didn't matter. He had blond, soft curls she tried now, looking at the car's charred body, not to imagine up in flames.

"That was in June '79," Junior says. He puts his foot up on the car's rusty bumper and it falls into the grass with a splintery crunch. He gives her a slit-eyed, assessing look, as if he is trying to place her.

"What?" Nan asks, and tips the beer back and finishes it. Junior doesn't seem to mind. He moves along again, down the rows of cars and stops.

"And this one," he says. He looks up, expecting she has followed him, but she has not. "Another of your *beaus*?" He says the word with a lilting, sarcastic edge. Nan does not want to acknowledge if it is or isn't. The sun slips behind clouds.

"Broder's Nova," he says.

John Broder, she thinks, who once held her down on the carpet in his father's apartment when she had been too drunk on blackberry brandy to protest. He died, like his father, of a bullet to the brain. He parked the Nova behind the old Grand Union. It was summer and two days before they found him, the car humming with flies. From her distance, Nan can see the car, not so deteriorated, its paint simply faded. Perhaps the inside is messy and hard to look at. Nan stays where she is. Junior watches her from behind his stringy hair.

"There's more," he says, like a game show emcee. She thinks she hears laughter in his voice.

Nan tries to smile. "I'll bet," she says. She holds the empty bottle out and Junior comes over to her and takes it from her hand. His boots flatten the dry grass. Small gnats flit around their ankles. It is late afternoon. Maybe early evening, she does not know. Through the ring of elms is someone's backyard, and she smells the burning of charcoal briquettes, hears children splashing in a pool. She imagines Clemmy with his cousins in her father's yard. They gather cut grass and arrange it in circles to make nests. They outline paths from one nest to the other, a whole interconnecting world made of her father's grass. She doesn't know how Clemmy will be with them, if he will play, like the other children, or sit quietly, morose, waiting for her to return. She asks Junior if she may use the restroom, and he leads her back into the garage to a small door. In the bathroom is a weak bulb with a dangling cord that Junior reaches past her to pull. Nan steps inside and closes the door. The plumbing is rusted, the toilet without a seat. She hovers over the bowl to relieve herself, gripping the rim. She rinses her hands in a grimy sink. There is no mirror for Nan to see what she looks like, but she feels her flushed cheeks, her hair flattened and damp. She remembers when, as a teenager, she experienced this same rushing feeling, as if each moment precipitated some culminating event.

When she emerges, Junior is waiting in front of the door. Beyond him the afternoon light shifts in waving patterns around the trunks of the elms. She and Junior look at each other. Nan wants to ask him what good it is to keep the cars here. But then he reaches out and takes her hand in his. It is warm and chalky, and surprisingly strong. He pulls her outside, along the first row to a Firebird convertible—the canvas top folded down, the seats in fairly good shape. Junior opens the passenger door and she hesitates.

"You've never done it in this one," he says. His voice is low and laughing.

Nan sits down on the seat and pulls her legs up to avoid the mildewed floorboard carpet. Junior leaves the door open and goes back to the garage. He returns with more beer in its cardboard holder and sets it on the console between the bucket seats. He climbs into the driver's side and pushes in the car's lighter. It pops out, glowing, and he lights his cigarette. The radio works, too, and he ejects an old eight-track tape from the player—*Canned Heat,* and holds it up for her to see, grinning. Nan can't imagine what she is doing there. She thinks that now, at her father's house, the children are organizing games of freeze tag or Mother-May-I? on the front lawn. Her father and sisters sit around their kitchen table, wondering what has become of her. Rose tapping her cigarette ash into the beanbag ashtray, assuring her father that Nan has gone to the mall in Farmington or to an old friend's. May more uncertain, declaring Nan knows no one in town anymore. The talk will shift to the trouble Nan had always gotten into, the way she left home, the barn. She imagines her sisters sharing a secret look.

Nan thinks she will stay with Junior as long as he will let her. It will grow dark, the fireflies emerging like burning batting, the stars bedding down overhead. They'll listen to the frogs in Filley Pond, a rolling sound, like a die in a tumbler. He might put his arm around her, and she will lean into his chest, into the smell of his T-shirt—a scent she identifies with the boys of her youth, mechanic's grease and sweat and cheap cologne Junior tries to play the tape, but it only works for a few minutes before it becomes garbled and breaks in the player. The sun sets with a vivid spray behind the trees, and they drink the beer.

"I've been working on this one," Junior tells her. He runs his fingers around the steering wheel.

"Why this one?" Nan asks.

"It's a good year," he says. "A '76."

Nan shrugs. She stares through the windshield as if they are heading somewhere.

"A lot happened that year," Junior says. He makes a humming noise under his breath. He leans against the driver's side door and looks over at her. His face is lined, she sees. Years have passed since he was a teenager. "Do you remember when the old Henley barn burned? Wasn't that in '76?" The cicadas whine, long, and high-pitched. Nan sighs.

"Do you know the story of the barn?" she asks.

"I think I've heard it," he says. The smoke from his cigarette spirals in the twilight.

Nan didn't think anyone else knew the story. But of course, Matt was Junior's friend, and he had told him. And who else, she wonders. Most likely everyone, she realizes. She had been foolish, assuming boys would care for her and keep her secrets. As if sex were a pact, a sealed envelope. She and Matt had lain in the moldy straw, and she had seen bats dart in and out of the eaves on their leathery wings. She had taken Matt's lighter from his jeans pocket to light her cigarette, and it had burned her thumb, and she dropped it. Matt scooped it up, but not before the flame caught. They got out, stumbling, laughing, in awe of the blaze, running back through the field to the safety of the tall pinewoods. Pieces of ash floated down around them. She watched the fire department put it out and imagined her sisters gathering with her father, her absence felt. Rose said their father cried with his face in his hands. May said they all cried, each hiding it from the other.

Nan had thought the fire beautiful. She watched with Matt, her mouth sore and reddened, her shirt open and her hair singed. Once, she told him, they had a swing from the rafters, and their mother would push them. They stored the apple crates in the barn, and the ladders the hired men used to harvest the orchard. Back then, the hay was freshly mown and sold to local farmers, the bales of it stacked in sweet smelling corded piles. Nan loved the barn with a childish, whimsical heart. But she knew it was all gone long before it burned. She had given up listening for her mother's footsteps on the landing outside her bedroom. She stopped believing she might catch sight of her at the kitchen counter. How silly, she thinks now, to imagine there might have been some mistake. Her mother died in a hospital, under a light the color of yellowed scotch tape. Nan was there to see her mother's pale face slacken, her lips drop open. She watched her father pack her mother's nightgowns in a suitcase and take them home.

"Story goes you were great in the hay, but careless with the lighter," Junior says.

She nods, thoughtfully. She never understood, until now, Matt's honest refusal to say he loved her.

"You remember me," she says. She pulls on the rearview mirror and looks at herself. "I'm the age of my mother when she died."

But she looks nothing like that face on the hospital pillow. She has her father's features—sharp nose and chin, confused, searching eyes. Now, in her childhood bedroom, Clemmy will be put to bed with her father's dry kiss on his forehead. The cut grass smell clings to his damp skin. The beetles beat at the metal screen. The light is soft and precious. Nan knows that warm lurch of lucky love. She cannot understand why it has never been good enough. Junior reaches out and puts a hand on her ankle. She feels his fingers encircle it, closes her eyes and hears the car upholstery crunch, feels his breath on her cheek as he leans in. This is how it was with boys. She tasted the beer on their lips, the aftershave on their roughened necks. There were others she'd been with who died, tragically, before their time. Paul Gerardi, of a long illness unnamed in the newspaper. They slept in the blue television glow of his basement room, while outside snow fell and buried her car. He hid her keys so she wouldn't leave, or spiked her drink with Demerol. Joseph Reynolds fell from the bow of his boat; his body tangled in the seaweed off Block Island. His hands were always busy, his voice cajoling. She let him carve his initials with his penknife on her shoulder.

Nan thinks Junior will kiss her, but he does not, so she kisses him instead. Her mouth blooms under his. She presses herself against him, bones, skin, fabric. Her hands slip down to undo his pants. The places on her body wait for his hands to find them. Then, he takes her shoulders and pushes her back. Nan hears herself make a sharp little noise of protest.

Junior gazes at her. His eyes are pools deeper and darker than that afternoon in the hazy sunlight. "I don't want anything from you," he says, matter-of-factly.

And it is true. She discovers him, small and soft as a baby's hand. The air stills, flattened by their defeated breath. Around them the old hulls ease themselves into the dirt. The elm leaves shiver. The car lighter pops out, and Junior raises its glowing end to his cigarette. Nan sees his eyes, absent of trickery. His silence settles around them, patient, and absolving. There is nothing left but to drive back to her father's house, warily, up and down the narrow roads, past the tall corn crowded in the fields like spectators and the shadows of barns that have yet to burn. It is their deaths, she thinks, that make them alive. There is the silver lighter flicking open again, a smell of butane. A hand on a stick shift, the knuckles' ridge. The smooth seams of workpants, the stubborn zippered fly of old jeans. She sees narrow hipbones under her own hands, the way her hair falls to cover his face. There are no lights and the stars are out, the night air on bare limbs, or worn sheets and the hum of motel air conditioning. Nan is the only repository of these memories. She drives and imagines that with lungs full of seawater, at the moment of the gun's report, engulfed in heat, on the last exhale, in a synapse spark she occurred to them: her skin, her long arms encircling them, her body surrendered, abject, something they never could forget.

galatea

I married William in upstate New York before he turned out to be the Collegetown Creeper. I took his last name and became Margaret Mary Bell. I was named after my father's cousin, a wayward nun, who as a novice with the Benedictine Sisters of Regina Laudis took off with three other sisters for a mission in California and was never heard from again. I often imagined them driving in a sky-blue sedan with the windows down and the bright sun on the hood. The air on their faces is cool and smells of wild flowers blooming in the highway median. It catches in their wimples, invades the seams and soothes their scalps. Their habits flap. They have the radio on, and the Searchers sing "Love Potion Number Nine," and the sisters laugh. They are young women, wedded to God. Their mouths open and drink in the sun and the wind. Under the black fabric their bodies surge in secret, betraying their vows. Sometimes, I wanted to be pinioned in that faith, in the rules of their love. I felt my heart drawn out in wild longing with the words: *devotion, ecstasy, rapture,* and *betrothal.*

I was going to graduate school then, and writing, and I met William Bell one day while my sister was visiting, and we went to a park playground by Cayuga Lake. The lake was dark and cold, and the wind gusted off of it in an unfriendly way, rattling the bare maple branches, clanking the chains of the mostly empty swings. The playground was the old-fashioned kind, with wooden seesaws and one of those spinning platforms with metal handles, and the few kids there were playing on that, all of them running in the worn circle of dirt, making it spin, feebly, and then jumping on. My sister and I didn't have children ourselves, but we remembered how fun it was when we were small, and so we told them to climb on and we both grabbed one of the metal bars, and the kids held on with their mittens, and we ran and pushed with all our force. Some of the kids were too small, and the spinning made them afraid, and one even flew off. It was a sickening sight, the way he was flung into the dirt. My sister and I looked at each other in horror, and a few of the other mothers knelt down by the boy, who turned out to be William Bell's nephew, and I almost cried I was so embarrassed. Then William came over and grabbed the boy by the arm and righted him, quickly, as if nothing was wrong.

"God, don't hate me," I said.

William had one of those smooth-cheeked faces that flush in cold weather. He brushed the dirt from the boy's pants knees, and wiped his tear-stained face with his bare hand, and the whole time he kept glancing up at me, reassuring me no, really, not a big deal. Meanwhile the little boy whimpered, and I wondered if he'd bumped his head or sustained some injury of which William remained oblivious.

"Is he OK?" I asked. And sure enough his pants had torn, and his little knee was skinned and raw and bloody.

"Oh, shit," William said. "My sister will kill me."

The other mothers had silently reclaimed their children, and none of us really knew how to tend to the boy, so William had to take him home that way and suffer his sister's anger. He told me about it that night when he called me, how his sister's eyes panicked, and she grabbed the boy away from him so quickly he felt like a criminal.

"You should have told her it was my fault," I said. I sat on my bed, pulled out from the couch. It had begun to snow. In the streetlight, I could see the snow whitening the branches of the big elm outside my window. I had written my phone number on a ski tag I tore from my sister's parka that afternoon. I was so happy he had called. I kept remembering his eyes looking at me in the park and the way his cheeks reddened from the cold. My sister sat watching TV a few feet away from me, shushing me every so often so she could hear. We drank hot chocolate spiked with Kahlua and ate candy corn I bought in a moment of nostalgia on Halloween. I told William about my Women and Grief course, how we listened to tapes of keening women from Ireland and Greece.

"I can barely stand it," I said.

"Is it sad?" he asked me. "Is it awful?"

I tried to explain how it was so awful I wanted to laugh, and how hard it was not to, did he think I was crazy? He told me no, of course not. "You're interesting," he said. He lived with his sister and his nephew, and was in-between jobs because he'd been kicked out of the university's College of Engineering. He was an inventor, he said, who could not abide by someone else's schedule. He called every day that week, and our talking became whispered intimations, everything taking on some imagined double meaning. He said my eyes were the color of moss on the rocks at the bottom of a shallow stream, and asked if he could come over to my apartment, and I remembered he had called me *interesting*, so I said yes.

He came on a Friday night. I watched for him out of my window, through the branches of the elm. My apartment was only one large room upstairs in a house on Seneca Street. Downstairs lived a poet named Angela who was a student, too. She was very tall and soft-spoken, one of those people you sit with late at night and tell everything to. I could see the light from her window, the way it shone out onto the snow. I often imagined what it would have been like to live in the entire house alone, to move freely through all the rooms, to traverse the stairs and wander into a dining room and a kitchen at the back of the house. Now, someone living a separate life occupied these spaces—Angela, and Geoff and his dog Suzie downstairs, and Professor Harrow upstairs with me. Our lives invaded each other's in unwanted, unacknowledged ways. The floors were oak and creaky, and I listened to Professor Harrow's insomniac footsteps back and forth when I couldn't sleep. I had a fireplace in my apartment. Angela had one downstairs in hers. We were not allowed to use them, but we lit large pillar candles in them, which gave the illusion of the warmth that we desired.

The cold here was bitter. Outside the city the wind spilled across sweeping, open spaces dotted with abandoned farm machinery, and old houses buckling in on themselves. You wouldn't think they were habitable, but once in a while there would be a tacked-up sheet in the doorway, or plastic nailed over the windows, and the pale spiral of smoke from a chimney. William Bell is not from anywhere else. He was born here, in Tompkins County, and lived here all his life. At one time his father sold and repaired lawnmowers in a shop behind their house, and before that he was an attorney. They had an enclosed front porch with an air hockey game, and a gnome statuary on the front lawn that William, as a child, believed came alive at night. Before she died his mother grew apples and sold them from a small roadside stand, McCoun and Winesap and Cortland. I imagined, from these aspects of his life, that I knew everything about him. When he pulled up to the curb I found myself rushing down the stairwell to meet him at the door, tugging him by the arm in from the cold. It was still snowing, the light, fluttery, lake effect snow that went on for days. "Come here, you," I said. He smiled, slowly, unsure what to make of me. His cheeks held their usual flush. He wore a wide-brimmed beaver-skin hat. We stood on the old worn Persian rug in what once was the vestibule. The walls were papered in brown, with tiny pink roses. The woodwork was brown, too, mahogany shining in the weak, yellow light. There was a coatrack and an umbrella stand and a small, rickety antique table. The whole downstairs smelled of Angela's incense.

He looked around, somewhat sheepishly, and removed his hat with one hand, grabbing it at the crown. "I like this place," he said, nodding.

"Your hat is different," I told him.

He looked at it in his hand. "Well," he said. "It was my father's hat."

When he glanced up at me his face was sad. Once, I thought, women met their lovers here and pressed by decorum demurely took their hats and coats. I wondered if those women had ever thought, like I did, that sex might add some sweet dimension of loss and sorrow conquered for a moment. I didn't know this person I had become. I had always assumed I would demand things of boys and men, bargain with my body, holding out until they proved themselves in some way. But that night, I didn't wait to kiss him. I wanted to ease that sadness about his mouth with mine. His lips clung and trembled, kissing me back. Upstairs in my apartment, by the wavering fireplace candlelight, I undressed for him. All year, except in July and August when the summer heat rose to make a sweltering pocket, my apartment was cold. William slid his hands up and down my body and felt the raised bumps on my skin. "I can't warm you up," he said. So we climbed into my bed under the quilt and the blanket. That night the palms of his hands skimmed the surface of me, and he talked, his voice a soft hum that I had grown used to on the phone. I didn't know what he wanted with me. When I touched him he took my hands away, sweetly, like a correcting parent. Then he fell asleep.

My bed was lumpy with springs, and I had a certain angle in which I slept. But with William taking up the space, and my body burning and bright from his fingertips, I could not. I imagined I was Sister Margaret Mary, who at my age entered the abbey. I'd always pictured her alone in her chaste bed, consumed with desire for something ineffable and bodiless, but lying there I knew you could not separate the two—body and desire. I watched the shadows of the elm on my white plaster wall. I listened to the silence of the snow. The branches, sheathed in ice, clicked together like delicate bones. I listened for Professor Harrow's slippered footfalls, their shuffle across his oak flooring, back and forth: sometimes, a deliberate, thoughtful pacing, and other times, a slow, anguished dragging. I rarely saw him in our upstairs hall. When I did, I must have worn an expression of sympathy, because he avoided me, and hurried down the stairs as if he knew I knew and was ashamed of his wakefulness. The times we met, his face was white and startled. His hair was damp, combed back. He wore a camel overcoat with soiled elbows and smelled of the cigarettes I'd seen him smoke furtively, like a teenager, at his cracked window.

On the first night William slept with me, Professor Harrow was quiet. I envied him. I tried to breathe in and out, regularly, to feign sleep. I propped my head in my hands and looked at William Bell's face. Were we still strangers? I wondered. Or had something been forged about which we would never speak? I wouldn't know just then how he felt. His sleeping, slack expression revealed nothing, and I felt a small stone of fear. How easily I could be abandoned. At least, in sleep, I would not have to wonder what I wanted. When I did sleep, it was near morning. I awoke to find William Bell watching me in the gray light. We were like sentries who had traded places.

I looked at him looking at me. He seemed sad again, defeated.

"You could never love me," he said, somberly.

His cheeks were flushed again. His breath came out in a white cloud, and the candles in the fireplace had burned down to flat saucers of wax. He sat upright with his bare chest exposed, and my grandmother's crocheted afghan swaddling his waist, multicolored and garish.

"Well," I said. I didn't know how to finish. I could not admit that I was thinking about his body below the covers. "You look cold."

He stared at me, his chest pale against the afghan. "I don't care," he said. "I don't care about anything right now."

He looked away. I heard him breathe deeply. But he didn't make a move to get up and leave. "You don't have to stay," I said. I rolled away from him to the metal edge of the bed. I thought of Professor Harrow waking, what his routine might be on a Saturday morning—toast, coffee in a china cup. I imagined him with buttery crumbs on his fingers, listening through the walls. William Bell sighed again and heaved himself out of bed. He was tall, and I heard his body unfold. I listened to him find his clothes, to his soft sighs retrieving them, and the sound of the fabric slipping over his arms and legs. Finally, he put on his shoes, big boots that clomped, one after the other on the wood floor. I turned around and he was standing over the bed.

"Tell me not to go," he said.

"Tell me you want to stay," I told him.

"Ask me to kiss you," he said.

"Do you want to kiss me?" I was confused. I saw it was useless to talk.

"I want to kiss you more than anyone I have ever met," he said, but he made no move toward the bed. His eyes were troubled and dark. He turned then and went out the door. I heard him thump down the stairs. I didn't get up and lock the door behind him. I lay there for a long time wondering whether or not to believe him. Finally, I slept again. When I awoke it must have been early afternoon. Weak sunlight shone across the end of the bed. And William Bell was there, sitting in the armchair I had found in an antique store, its worn upholstered arms curving over wood inlaid with the carved heads of ducks. He was watching television without the sound. He ate from a carton I recognized from the Korean place in Collegetown. I thought I should be a little afraid of him, coming into my apartment without asking, but I was not.

I moved on the bed, and he glanced back at me. He smiled, wide and happy. I hadn't seen him smile like that before. There were many things I hadn't seen about him, things I couldn't know. None of that mattered then. My body was warm, my limbs slid across the soft sheets. He brought the food over to the bed and sat on the end.

"Are you hungry?" he asked. I rose up onto my knees and put my arms around his shoulders. His face changed, quickly, like clouds moving over the sun and the shadows lengthening on a lawn. He set the food down on the floor. I smelled its spices on his mouth. I heard his breathing catch, felt his body's sudden shift, its tension, like something coiled and tight. His hands were cold. It felt wonderful, his hands on me, his mouth moving, his groans. I thought: he came into my room while I slept, and I grew breathless and greedy for him.

We stayed in bed all that day. I heard Professor Harrow come up the stairs and slip his key into his lock. William Bell held me in his hands. I felt my body transform, heighten and strain and sigh. What else would make me happier? The light moved in its pale way across the foot of my bed, across the worn oak floor. It settled in the lap of the antique chair. We let the room grow dim and darken and match the outside. When the streetlight came on, we watched the snow falling in it.

"Does it ever stop snowing here?" I asked him. His hand was heavy, pressed to my bare stomach.

"It's winter," he said, as if this was an answer.

My stomach rumbled, and he said we needed to feed me, and so he pulled me up and my nakedness was light and airy in the dark. I stood on the foldout bed. He slid off the end and stood in front of me.

"Look at you," he said. "Galatea."

I posed, rigid, like marble.

William Bell reached up and put his hands on my hips. I remembered this moment for a long time after—the press of his thumbs, his cradling of me. He leaned in and kissed my hipbones, my thighs. I didn't need food. I wanted to be ravished. This was, for the most part, what became of us: his devotion, my submission. That night we dressed and went out into the snowy street. The houses lined up in their rows, their roofs thick and white, the lampposts and power lines and tree limbs all leaden with snow. The snow falling was eerie and oddly warm. He held my hand, and I let him. Every so often he stopped and pulled me in to kiss. A passing car's headlights would light us up.

"Isn't this being in love?" he said.

I told him I didn't know.

We stood on the sidewalk, under someone's porch light. Inside the house we saw people watching television, just their feet in socks propped up on a coffee table. They still had their jack-o-lanterns on the porch. Nearly buried, you could just make out the carved grimaces. I noticed, all around, things caught unprepared by snow—a rake propped on a fence, a child's bicycle tossed down on the grass. On the porch a pair of socks, pulled off and abandoned, frozen stiff in its contortions.

"You don't trust anything," he said, despondent. He let my hand drop. I had to retrieve his hand and tell him to stop it. I wondered if this was love, this constant reclamation, this rush to reassure. We kept walking and he steered me past the railroad tracks, into an end of town I had never been, not even with Angela in her Volvo. We stopped at the head of a path. Below us a creek, not yet frozen, rushed in the dark. To the right were scattered twinkling lights, and a soft din of conversation. I sensed low-built dwellings coated with snow and imagined people in them. There were several fires burning. The place smelled of wood smoke and the dank creek mud.

William Bell took my hand. "Let's go," he said.

Of course, I would not. He looked back at me, calmly chastising. "These people know me," he said.

My feet had grown cold in my boots. I didn't know what he would need to say to make me walk down the path with him. He stepped toward me and slid his two hands up under my coat, under my sweater and T-shirt. His hands on my skin, the press of his fingertips, were somehow consoling, familiar.

"You must trust me," he said, softly, into my hair.

And I was not sure whether it was that I trusted him, or that I worried if I didn't, he would take his hands away forever. He held my hand again and we went down the path worn muddy by other's footsteps. The enclave consisted of tents and tarps strung on two-by-fours. Strung bulbs or Christmas lights, powered by small generators, lit some of the dwellings. There were end tables with small, shaded lamps and tinny radios. Under the tarps or around the fires, the people sat in aluminum chairs, the kind with plastic slats, low-slung canvas chairs, camp chairs, the type you took to an outdoor concert or a kid's sports game, or the beach. The people eyed us warily. They were dressed for the weather, in layers of clothes that made them look lumpy, and all of the same size and sex. We kept walking down the narrow paths. The snow fell, landing in their fires, and hissing. The mud sucked at my boots. From the tents came the smells of stale breath, refuse, dirty clothes hampers. We arrived at a fire removed from the others. Around it, the people laughed and passed a bottle around. They smoked, and their exhaling formed large clouds about their heads. When they saw William, they greeted him all at once.

"Well, if it isn't Mr. Bell Jr." one said.

There were no chairs for us. We stood beside their group, feeling the warmth of their fire on our faces.

"What do you have for us?" someone else asked. I wondered if this was a kind of password, or mode of entry, the bringing of something, like a gift. I still could not distinguish between the men and the women. Their voices were the same—deep and gravelly. They wore knitted caps, some with pompoms, some striped and bright. They seemed like children sitting by the fire.

"I've brought the woman I'm going to marry," William said.

I looked at him, quickly, and stepped away. "What?" I said.

There was a sudden quiet. A throat was cleared, raspy, horrible. Either William's announcement, or my objection, was out of place in their circle. I thought I saw one person roll their eyes.

"Oh Lord, get Billy Bell out here," another said.

Around us the snow blew softly. The sky was a black bowl, starless. I could see the shapes of trees, their remaining leaves withered and clinging, lonely shapes on slender twigs. A man emerged from one of the nearby tents. He was tall and well-built. He wore a heavy tweed overcoat and lumbered up to us. In the firelight, I saw his eyes in his roughened face that were exactly like William Bell's.

"What now?" he said, gruff, unforgiving.

He pulled out a cigarette from his pocket and then looked to the group for a light. William took a silver Zippo from his own pocket and lit the man's cigarette. Both of their hands went up to cup the flame from the wind. Here was the man who lined up mowers on his front lawn with prices handwritten on cardboard placards, who with youthful earnestness argued cases in a courtroom in downtown Ithaca. I noticed he was unsteady, swaying in his long coat.

"Did you hear?" someone around the fire said. "He's brought the woman he is going to marry."

"Or not," snickered someone else. The group laughed, tentatively, not sure of what to make of this situation.

The tall man sighed. He wore a wool Burberry's scarf tucked into his collar. He would not look at either of us.

"Get out of here," he said, quietly. His voice was ominous, threatening.

William Bell stayed. They were nearly the same height.

"I thought you should meet," he said. I sensed the sarcasm in his voice, a kind of tremor. I saw that once, the older man would have put his hand on William's shoulder, or taken him in his arms. I knew that William was waiting for all of these things.

Someone in the circle started singing a low, bawdy song. Something about *wedded* and *bedded, O.* Others joined in, creating a distraction, an odd background accompaniment. The older man turned and stumbled back into his tent. I figured he would have his place to sit there, his bottle. He could listen to our retreating footsteps in the mud and feel whatever it was he felt—compunction, sorrow. As we left, the other groups around their fires joined in the song. There was cackling laughter, not derisive, but a waylaid sadness. I imagined all of them having slipped down their own lives to this place, forsaken, or perhaps unwilling to let anyone lay claim to them. We made our way up the embankment, listening to the creek slough its banks. Soon, the temperature would dip and its surface would still and thicken. Underneath the rainbow trout would sit, dumb and cowed, waiting for spring.

I did not talk about the incident of that evening to William Bell. We returned to my apartment and it was dawn. We walked home in silence. I held his hand. Upstairs we met Professor Harrow in his plaid robe and slippers. His ankles were bare and white. He seemed dazed, standing on the landing. It was cold, and our breath came out around our heads.

"Good morning," he mumbled, standing there as if he'd been chased from his room by something to which he did not wish to return. I put my key in the lock and regretted seeing him like that. Inside the apartment it was still cold, still gray and dark.

William Bell sat heavily on the end of the bed and put his face in his hands. The elm scraped my window. The snow fell, invisibly, blending into the whitish morning. I sat down beside William and felt I might save him with a profession of love. I pushed him down on the bed and looked into his face. He shook his head and tried to turn away.

"Look at me," I said, and he did.

We looked at each other for a long time, believing we knew what the other thought. I saw I could imagine anything about him, even a past he might never confess. I saw this was what love was.

"Will you?" he asked.

I kissed him. His hands fell back into place on my body. We both got what we wanted, I think. A notary in an old house on Tioga married us in a civil ceremony. Outside, the snow was like powdered sugar falling through a sieve. It didn't seem real. It was like stage snow, pretty and harmless. As we spoke our vows, though, it turned to ice, and slanted against the window, a vindictive tapping.

We had very little money. He worked for a few weeks at Agway, selling snow shovels and bags of salt and light bulbs, and I was proud of him, getting up at a normal hour, showering and putting on clean clothes. He came home sedate and smelling like a springtime lawn, and I was happy. Then he quit. He acquired and left a succession of jobs, and I discovered that this was his pattern, and he saw nothing wrong with it. I stayed with him in Ithaca for the Christmas holiday. His sister had been furious when she'd found out we'd married, and she refused to have anything to do with us, so I hadn't, yet, told my own family. It seemed then the most foolish of things to do with my life.

We fell into a kind of decline. The apartment was cluttered and unclean. I had a small stove and a few pots that we washed out when we needed them. They sat on the burners with their previous contents congealing. William's bits of magnetized wire, bulbs, circuits, and metal shavings littered the window ledges. The little Christmas tree still sat in its pot on the table by the window, its branches absent of any green life. The glass ornaments slipped off, one at a time at night. In the darkness, they made small splashing sounds when they shattered, like spilling water.

Winter in upstate New York is interminable. The snow was a burden in piled banks, an endless tumbling of flakes. Icicles hung from the house's eaves, deadly threats you ducked under, or knocked off with a shovel. The reaches of snow were vast, wide, white fields rolling on and on. There was a bitter wind that rattled the windows in their frames. I didn't think I could stand it, and I told William Bell, and he gave me his look of reproof. *Consider the people in the encampment,* his look said. We had not gone back there again, though I suspected that William did. When we shopped at Goodwill, looking for a writing table, he purchased clothing and shoes that I never saw him wear. Often, Angela offered us food, extra loaves of bread, casseroles in disposable tins, and it disappeared. I didn't question him about anything. I let the undiscussed spaces in our life together flourish. I didn't care where he went or what he did, as long as he returned to me.

And then one afternoon I came home and the chairs that went around my small table were missing. Another day the lamp was gone, and then the table itself. These things were not acceptable, I told him. He stared at me, blankly, with his beautiful flushed cheeks. He did not return that night, or the next, or the next, when the snow stopped, and things began to melt and drip. I called his sister but hung up on the answering machine. For two weeks I went to my classes, and came home, and he was still gone. I began to imagine Sister Margaret Mary, just before her flight, her unrequited body prone on her narrow bed in her sparsely furnished room. There was her dark clothing in the closet, and above the small chest of drawers the brassy body of Christ on the cross, the object onto which she safely fastened her own longing. And then I came back from class one evening and the hangers that once held his clothes were bare wires, and the bureau drawer where he kept his sweaters and balls of socks was empty.

I distracted myself with cleaning, left the windows open and let the cold air blow through the place. I brushed William's magnetized pieces of wire and metal out the window into the snow below. I used bleach and scrubbed, borrowed Angela's mop. I loaded the blankets and sheets in her car and drove them to the Laundromat, maneuvering around the potholes in the streets, the slush spraying up onto the windshield. Outside, without William Bell, the world was changing.

At the Laundromat, I saw a boy I'd met when I first came to school. I could not remember his name, but he remembered mine, and he asked me what I was reading, and what courses I was taking this semester, and then asked me more things, and I realized I wasn't answering him the way I normally might because I was married now, and I felt the boundaries of this without really wanting to. The big hot dryers rolled and tumbled. Pieces of lint floated past. And I looked at his earnest expression, his eyes lit with genuine interest, and I looked at myself as he saw me: my hair too long, uncombed, my sweater with its unraveling wool hem, the smell of bleach on my hands. And I wondered, crazily, if he could love me. "Help me take my stuff to my car," I said.

He grabbed armfuls. I opened the Volvo's trunk and we put the sheets and blankets inside. And then we stood in the slush in the cold, filling the space between us with our fogging breath. "Come home with me and help me make the bed," I said.

He glanced around, as if someone might witness all of this occurring, as if he'd stepped into a story and been asked to play a role. He didn't smile and answer right away. Then I saw him bite the inside of his cheek.

"Are you serious?" he said, quietly, covertly.

I shrugged. "Of course," I told him.

Climbing into his car he was eager and quick. He drove that way, too, following too close behind, almost hitting me once at a stop sign. At my house I parked at the curb and he carried everything in his arms up the stairs. His footsteps were light, glancing off each step, careening up to the landing where he had to wait for me to unlock the door. I heard him breathing behind the pile of laundry.

Inside, the breeze had whipped things into a frenzy. Magazines and manuscript pages had blown onto the floor. The curtains were caught up in their rods. All of the old smells seemed resurrected—fireplace ashes, oak polish, the walls' dampened plaster. It wasn't unpleasant. It felt cold and fiercely alive.

"It is freezing in here," the boy said.

I imagined he dreaded removing his clothes.

I shut the windows and the room stilled. I turned to him and tried to remember his name. We were in the Native American class on the third floor of the Andrew White house. We read the story of the Lakota. He grinned at me from across the room. I saw he had no idea what to do, and without any complicity, neither did I.

"This is the bed," I said. The mattress was thin in the pitiless March light. He grabbed an end of a sheet, and we stretched it out from either side. From the pile of bed sheets we found the one to go on top, our heads bumping, sorting through everything. His hair smelled of shampoo. The room filled with the smell of clean laundry. We made the bed. He was very competent and serious, as if this was really what he had expected. When we were done he sat down on the edge.

"I want a cigarette," he said. He looked up at me, apologetically.

"I don't smoke," I told him. I sat down on the bed next to him.

"Maybe we should go out and have a few pitchers of beer," he said.

I took his hand and placed it on my leg. We both looked at it, a fine hand with long fingers and bulky knuckles. "There isn't a set way to go about this," I told him. "Either you want me more than a cigarette, or you don't."

He chuckled and ran his free hand through his hair. He would not look at me at all. "Do you do this a lot?" he asked. "I mean you're a pretty girl. I could be the Creeper."

I asked him what he meant, and he told me the story of the Collegetown Creeper, how he showed up in women's unlocked apartments while they slept. They awoke to him standing over their beds, or sitting idly in a chair wearing a wide-brimmed hat. I imagined they did not look favorably on his presence or invite him to bed. They screamed, and swore at him, and called the authorities. I looked at the boy's fine-boned face, his eyebrows drawn together, telling his story.

"You aren't him," I said.

"Didn't you go to Wellesley?" he asked.

I told him he must have me confused with someone else.

"Didn't you go to Yale?" I asked him, playing along.

He laughed then. "No, I didn't," he said.

"Well then," I said. "We aren't who we thought we were."

The spot of sun on the bed was almost warm. "We are just imitations of what we thought," he said.

His hand on my leg heated it up. Our bodies touched at the shoulder and hip. They sank at varying depths into the too-thin mattress. "What if we kiss?" I suggested. Anything to stop his musing.

He put both of his hands on my face then and held it like a bowl you might tip and drink from. I felt my heart shift and give, dislodged from its winter hibernation. Most men exhibit at least one endearing gesture, and this was his. His mouth was soft and he closed his eyes. We kissed for a long time on the clean-smelling bed. He whispered my name like a summoning spell. I didn't even know his. I wouldn't have said it, anyway. I knew he wouldn't stay, that once he was through and his clothing back on he would saunter out into the hallway, relieved to be done with me, grateful and changed, but still relieved. It was this way with all of them afterward. When they left, they always gave me something. "You're sweet," they'd say. I'd have put on his undershirt, and when I began to remove it he'd tell me, "No, keep it." One gave me his St. Christopher's medal on a tarnished chain, another, his L. L. Bean windbreaker. Often, when they spent the night, I dreamed I heard William's boots clomping up the stairs, scraping mud outside the door. He would come in and stand by the bed in the gray light. I'd search his face for some evidence of my betrayal and find none. His eyes did their usual sad dance over the body he no longer held, and then he turned and left the room. Sometimes, in the dream, I chased after him. And sometimes, awake, I did the same, slipping out of bed and down the stairs, out the front door onto the porch. I'd stand there, shivering, half-dressed, fooled by what was dream and what was real, no longer able to tell the difference.

At Easter I finally went home to visit and when I returned to my apartment it had been emptied of its furnishings. Angela was out of town. When I knocked on Professor Harrow's door he answered and placed a hand on my arm. His eyes held a blinking lasciviousness I had never noticed before. "Well, well," he said, and I pulled my arm away. "I assumed you'd moved out." There had been banging on the stairs, he told me, and a pickup truck at the curb. I knew William Bell had been there and taken everything. I would not go looking. I did not trust what I wanted to find—my duck-carved chair inside the flap of a tent, its legs sunk in muddied earth, the bed unfolded from the couch in the broad spring sunlight. I might have begged to stay, to lie down on the worn sheets that smelled of melting snow. At night the little strung lights must leave spangles on the canvas like stars. The bonfire smoke invades clothing and pores. The creek rushes its banks again with fervor. I no longer remember the day we married, only the day I knew we would, those moments with my heart warm and rapt, the silent promise of the frozen world, the elm chafing in its coat of ice.

KAREN BROWN was born in Connecticut. Her stories have appeared in many literary journals including *Epoch, Alaska Quarterly Review, StoryQuarterly,* and *Tampa Review.* She received an O. Henry Prize for "Unction," originally published in *The Georgia Review* and included in *The O. Henry Prize Stories, 2006.* She lives in Tampa, Florida, with her husband and three children.